Praise for
ANN RINALDI'S
The Second Bend in the River

"As she did in *Wolf by the Ears* (1991), Rinaldi weaves a powerfully romantic tale of two Americans from the colonial era. Her attention to period details and careful separation of fact from fiction strengthen the credibility of the story without diminishing any of its appeal."

— *Booklist*

"Tecumseh's proposal of marriage, Rebecca's confusion and their final love scene will pull at all hearts that have felt the pangs of first love. Rebecca's shrewd observations, resourcefulness and compassion make her a character to be reckoned with — and one girls on the threshold of womanhood will appreciate."

— *Publishers Weekly*

"Rebecca is a strong-minded character with a believable and authentic voice. Anyone who enjoys historical fiction will find much to like about this well-written and carefully researched novel. A rewarding and satisfying read."

— *School Library Journal*

"Rinaldi follows the historical record closely. Only the dialogue and a handful of minor characters and incidents are fictional."

— *Kirkus Reviews*

Other POINT SIGNATURE paperbacks you will enjoy:

The Mozart Season
by Virginia Euwer Wolff

From the Notebooks of Melanin Sun
by Jacqueline Woodson

Dove and Sword
by Nancy Garden

Arilla Sun Down
by Virginia Hamilton

When She Hollers
by Cynthia Voigt

The Road Home
by Ellen Emerson White

POINT • SIGNATURE

THE *SECOND*

BEND

IN THE *RIVER*

ANN RINALDI

SCHOLASTIC INC.

New York   Toronto   London   Auckland   Sydney
Mexico City   New Delhi   Hong Kong

No part of this publication may be reproduced in whole or in part, or stored in a retrieval system, or transmitted in any form or by any means, electronic, mechanical, photocopying, recording, or otherwise, without written permission of the publisher. For information regarding permission, write to: Scholastic Inc., Attention: Permissions Department, 555 Broadway, New York, NY 10012.

ISBN 0-590-74259-0

Copyright © 1997 by Ann Rinaldi.
All rights reserved. Published by Scholastic Inc.
SCHOLASTIC and associated logos are trademarks
and/or registered trademarks of Scholastic Inc.

12 11 10 9 8 7 6 5 4   2 3 4/0

Printed in the U.S.A.   01

First Scholastic paperback printing, May 1999

Typeset in Goudy.

To Daniel,
my third grandson

THE SECOND BEND IN THE RIVER

The white-hot sky swirled overhead. Katydids droned the promise of even more heat. I squinted at the Indian. He seemed part of the trees, the undergrowth. Part of the landscape. Even part of the river and the sky. Like he belonged there.

I knew about Indians, all right. When my daddy was four years old back in Pennsylvania, his grandmother was killed by one when they burned out his town in the French and Indian Wars. He recollects a horse coming back to the blockhouse where they were holed up, all bloody and shot up, its rider missing and dead.

Then there was Nancy Maxwell, the sheriff's wife. Her father and only child were killed by Indians back in Virginia. She made bullets in the fort when they were being attacked. She told me about them smashing babies against the trees. Mama said it wasn't true. But I knew it was. Mrs. Maxwell wouldn't have that look in her eyes if it weren't.

Now we had an Indian here.

I minded Daddy's words. We were at peace with the Indians. It had to do with the Treaty of Greenville in 1795. The Indians agreed to do something. Or not to do something. Likely not to smash any more babies against trees. But I was still scared and needed, more than ever now, to pee.

I looked back at our house. It was made of hewn logs. And it sat on a rise of land, a quarter of a mile from the bend in the Little Miami River, smoke curling out of its two chimneys, like a satisfied hen keeping her eggs warm. It nestled there. Two stories. Solid and square. A mile from town. My brother George was sixteen when he helped Daddy build it. James was thirteen, but he helped, too.

It had a good view of the river, the distant mountain ranges, and our wide fields. A gathering of sugar maples cast shade in the back. The barn, corncrib, and outbuildings were close enough to seem part of it, without crowding.

But the sight of it gave me small comfort then with that Indian watching us.

From where I was standing I could hear Andrew being fretful inside the house. Would the Indians consider Andrew a baby? He was two. Hush, Andrew, I wanted to say. Then I heard John chanting a Scottish ditty. John was four. Would he get to keep his brains?

"Rebecca? You fetch those beans yet?" Mama's voice. It carried on the summer air. Oh, I was sure that Indian had heard it. I turned and ran toward the house. I dropped the beans. "Mama!" I ran inside. "Mama, there's an Indian out there watching us!"

Mama jiggled Andrew on her shoulder and peered out the window, which didn't have the oiled paper on it because of the heat. She didn't get quickened with fear. She stayed calm. Daddy said that she had the

4

appearance of authority. And she never laid it aside, no matter what.

"We'll have company for supper," she said.

"Company? An Indian?"

"Yes. He looks like the one who was here a year ago March when we first arrived. Your father spoke to him then and invited him back. Likely he's come now to visit."

Indians don't visit, I wanted to say. They attack. "Should I ring the dinner bell for Daddy?"

"No." She set Andrew down in the cradle, the new one brother George had made. Then she gathered up the basket with the vittles in it for me to take to my father and brothers in the fields.

"Go along now."

"You want me to walk out there alone? With that Indian skulking around?"

"He isn't skulking, Rebecca."

"What's he doing then?"

"Waiting for your father to come home. Your imagination is getting too lively. If you don't rein it in, I'll have to keep you from the books."

She knew that would shut my mouth, all right. Books were all I had out there in the wilderness. I lived for my time with our books. True, I'd have given a wall of them for a friend my age, who was a girl. Two walls for a sister. "Why do I have so many brothers?" I asked Mama once.

"It's the Lord's blessing, Rebecca."

Well, I could have done with a little less blessing. Especially the one named James. I'd have given him up in a minute for the older sister I dreamed about. She would have told me stories, helped me curl my hair. And she never would have swatted me. I took the basket and went out the door.

I stepped into the white-hot day. I gathered the world in with my eyes.

It looked like the quilt Mama was stitching. A patch of red for the barn, a border of brown for the zigzagged fencing my brothers had built from our walnut and hickory trees. Scraps the color of cream for the merino sheep. Dark splashes of color for the cattle. And some gold, too, the color of Shag's coat. Shag, our dog, who came all the way from Kentucky with us. More brown and white for brother Sam's dogs sleeping in their pen, all lean and ready for the hunt.

Oh, it was mortal sweet to the eye. Running creeks, salt licks, and over to Colonel Massie's place a wild vine sixteen feet around. Old sycamores so big farmers used them for hog pens. Everything you needed. But dangerous.

It could kill you, this world. Danger lurked everywhere. Armies of squirrels lay in wait for the corn. Foxes took poultry. Wolves ran off with colts and calves.

Clouds of migrant pigeons came out of the sky to

settle in the spring fields and eat the young sprouts. Sometimes my brothers had to wade through them, like you'd wade through blue-gray water, and hack away.

Deer crept under the moon to eat growing things. Green caterpillars quietly stripped the land.

"Why did we come here?" I'd ask Mama when I saw my father and brothers bone-weary from fighting all this.

"To get away from slavery," she'd answer.

To come into it, she should have said. My father and brothers weren't slaves in Kentucky. Here they were.

Shag followed me into the fields. The path was worn. My daddy and brothers were clearing some land, burning timber. Smoke filled the air. Piles of logs that weren't there this morning were ready to be taken to the sawmill.

When I got to the edge of the blackened stubble of a field, I turned and looked back.

That Indian was still standing under those trees.

Daddy walked halfway back to the house with me when they finished their noon meal. He shaded his eyes and peered. "It's Tecumseh," he said.

"What is he?"

"Shawnee."

"Shawnee killed Nancy Maxwell's father and baby."

7

"That was a long time ago, Rebecca. This one is civilized, friendly. When he was here last year he promised me no harm would come to us."

"Where was I when he came?"

"Sleeping. You had the fever, remember? Like the one that killed Joseph."

Joseph was birthed two years before me. He's buried back in Kentucky. I wasn't supposed to live through my fever, but I did.

Enough said. Dark clouds were threatening over the hills. They had to finish their work. I went back to the house.

When I got back Mama made me pick up the beans I'd spilled. Every one. "Waste not, want not," she said. She was very taken with Benjamin Franklin.

I ate my noon meal and played with John. When Andrew woke from his nap I took him outside under the trees in back.

That Indian stood there like a lost sheep the whole time.

It was my job to ring the dinner bell. When I stepped outside to do so, Shag was nervous. He barked, sharp and often, but Mama shushed him and brought him inside, where he stayed close as a cocklebur to me and the little ones.

Another job of mine was to fetch cool water in gourds for the menfolk. Being the only girl in the family was a plague. I fetched the water, then had to set the table.

"Set a bowl for our visitor," Mama said.

I stared at her like she was touched by the sun. Might have been. She'd spent the morning weeding the kitchen garden.

"He won't be able to sit at the table," I said.

"Do as you're told, Rebecca."

I set out the bowl. If the Indian was company, why wasn't she taking out her carpet. It was her one vanity. It had come from somewhere across the ocean when we were in Kentucky, and it had flowers on it. She spread it out over the wood floor when company came. She had branch candlesticks, too. But she didn't fetch them out, either.

I wished the Indian was real company. An old soldier, maybe. Then we'd hear stories about the war and how Daddy was in the fields of Pennsylvania when Captain Adams came and asked him to go against the British. And Daddy said he'd go when he finished the things he was at. And Captain Adams asked for the sickle. Daddy gave it and went home and made two pairs of moccasins, then marched the next day to Carlisle to meet with the others.

I wouldn't have even minded a landlooker for company, though then the talk would be all about the earth. Daddy and my brothers would talk about clay, loam, bogs, upland, good bottomland, and sloughs the livelong night.

If our visitor were a trapper, we'd hear about the fur posts in the West. Brother Sam would get a hungry look in his eyes at the strange-sounding names: Prairie du Chien, Green Bay, Peoria. Mama said that Sam, at eleven, was already gathering himself in to be a coming-and-going man.

The menfolk were washing up outside. My daddy, George, James, Sam, and Will. They were loud, sweaty, rough, and gentle all at the same time. There was a lot of talk and foolishment about the Indian from my brothers.

"What's he come for?" Sam asked.

George ruffled my hair. "To court Becca," he said.

"I'll get my tomahawk," from Will. He was better with the tomahawk than anybody.

Daddy shushed them. Then said he was going down to the river to invite the Indian in.

James didn't say anything. He let everybody else do the talking first. Foolishment wasn't his way. But he took his rifle down from the wall and set it nearby. He was pure daft over that rifle. It had a curly maple stock and brass fixings.

"Sit, everyone," Mama ordered.

We sat. Daddy came back, but not the Indian. "He's shy," Daddy said.

George laughed. Then Daddy looked at him and he

stopped. George was nineteen, the oldest. But Daddy's looks could still stop him.

Daddy said a prayer, and we ate. Then he spoke. "He once lived here. It was his village when he was a child. They had fields of corn right where we have ours. They are a proud people."

"Where does he live now?" Will asked.

"Sixty miles west in Indiana country."

"Why has he come?" from George.

"The land here means much to him," Daddy explained. "He has good memories. Like you all have of Kaintuck."

Daddy and my brothers called the place we came from Kaintuck. There was a bleak silence then, while each of us struggled with our memories. No matter what we called it, Kaintuck or Kentucky, it was home. I didn't know about the others, but I'd have gone right back. We'd had a real house in Kentucky. Brick. And friends. I went to school. We should have stayed. Daddy's friend Simon Kenton stayed, and he was a rich man.

I had a cat, gray and fluffy with green eyes. You couldn't take a cat over the mountains. Cats are for people who are settled and civilized. Indians have dogs but not cats. You have to earn the right, as a people, to have cats. And I'd have one again someday soon.

"Rebecca, ring the dinner bell again," Daddy said. "And leave the door open."

I did so. The sound rang out, clear and sweet. Then I sat back down at the table.

After about ten minutes a shadow fell across the room.

The Indian was in the doorway. He wore buckskins with some quillwork. And silver in his ears and on his arms. His hair was straight and sleek. A silver medallion hung on rawhide around his strong neck. His nose was long, his eyes sad. Around his head he wore a red band and into it was stuck an eagle feather.

I felt as if I was looking at something wild. Something forgotten. Yet at the same time, something not one of us could ever forget. And he was there to remind us of it, whatever it was.

Daddy stood up. "Welcome, Tecumseh. I'd be proud if you'd make yourself to home."

CHAPTER 2

Wait until I tell Mrs. Maxwell about this, I thought. She'll take to sleeping in the loft again, like she used to do so the Indians wouldn't kill her at night.

As soon as Tecumseh came into the room, everybody did what they did best. My brothers stood up and looked tall and ready for just about anything. Mama fetched him a bowl of soup. Shag barked. James ordered him to stop. Little John clung to George and put his thumb in his mouth. Baby Andrew stared.

I just sat there and shivered. It wasn't much of an accomplishment, but I could do it without letting anyone know I was scared.

"George, get the guest chair," Daddy said.

George brought forth the chair. It was straight-backed with firm arms, just like George himself. He made it of good sound hickory.

Tecumseh stood looking around for a moment. I saw his eyes take in the two rooms that made up the first floor of our house. The kitchen, with its huge hearth, the copper kettles and all Mama's pots, the trestle table and chairs. Then the other room, lined with shelves and shelves of Daddy's books.

He gestured. "Walls made of books," he said.

"You know about books?" Daddy asked.

"Talking leaves," he said. "Tecumseh can read little. And write little. Would learn more. Tecumseh knows about your Jesus God. And about Chief Hamlet."

"Chief Hamlet?" Daddy was puzzled for a minute. Then he smiled. "You mean Shakespeare's Hamlet?"

The Indian nodded vigorously. Then he smiled, and my brothers did, too.

Tecumseh looked at each of us in turn. "Thanks to you, good lady, for food," he said. Then he began to chant in Indian language. It was a lilting sound, and it made me shiver more. I felt like he was conjuring and soon there would be a whole bunch of Indians in the room. His eyes were closed.

And then it came to me what he was doing. Praying over the soup. "Thanks to Weshemoneto, the Great Father, for this food. And for bringing us together," he said.

14

I may have been young, but I knew things. I knew my Bible, my letters and sums. I could play the violin a bit, card wool, change the baby, put together a pie, and help make soap. Mama taught me all that. The rest of what I knew, I learned from my brothers. And from Mrs. Maxwell.

How to ride, tap sugar from a tree, load a gun, though I was too young to hold one, stitch a pair of moccasins. I knew that trees told what kind of land lay under them. White oaks and chestnuts meant land good for corn. Sassafras, small oaks, persimmon meant thin soil; hard maple meant rich ground begging for the seed.

I knew that a big walnut, cedar, or hickory tree could yield two hundred rails for fencing, that hogs were best slaughtered in the waxing moon or the bacon would shrivel, that Indians had a silver mine hidden somewhere, that you could get a bounty for killing wolves, foxes, and wildcats, but you first had to turn over their tongue and ears. I knew that the mail left Pittsburgh every Friday at two in the afternoon and came through our settlement, Chillicothe, the following Thursday.

I knew that Will, only thirteen, was already sweet on Elizabeth Pomeroy, the bound girl who lived one hour's ride north. And that Mama was to have another baby next spring. Though my brothers didn't know that yet.

But I never knew that Indians prayed before eating. James, who was holding Andrew on his lap, nudged me and whispered that I should stop staring. We commenced eating again. And if I was surprised at the prayer, I was more surprised that this Indian could pick up a pewter spoon and use it properlike. He ate the soup, nodding and smiling at Mama as he did so.

He never spilled a drop.

He ate the bread put before him, too. And the plate of boiled, buttered beans, the very ones I'd dropped and had to pick up earlier.

"Good," he pronounced. "Good very."

"Rebecca picked and cleaned and cooked them," Mama said.

He turned to look at me. The hazel eyes were like the sky after a good rain. He smiled at me. His teeth were very white.

"Good little straw-hair girl. How many summers?" he asked Mama. "Seven?"

"How did you know?" Mama asked.

He pointed to his teeth. Everyone laughed, and I blushed. Because of my missing teeth I couldn't say my words right, and it made me grievous uncomfortable.

The Indian smiled at me. "Say Tecumseh's name, little straw-hair girl."

"Tecumtha," I said.

Everyone laughed. But Tecumseh held up his hand. "That is right way to say my name. Because of her missing teeth, I knew she would say it so. She is the only white person who ever said it as it is meant to be."

"Tecumtha," my daddy said solemnly.

"Gal-o-weh!" Tecumseh said.

More laughter. After that it was better. But it still didn't feel right, having an Indian sitting at table with us. I thought about Daddy's grandmother, killed by one back in Pennsylvania. And wondered if he was thinking on that now. But apparently he wasn't. I helped Mama clear the table and brought over the huckleberry pie I'd made early that morning under Mama's supervision.

Tecumseh ate some pie. "Good," he said, "good very."

"Rebecca made it," Mama said again.

I wished she wouldn't single me out. I'd just as soon they all forgot me.

"Little straw-hair girl." Tecumseh nodded. And then he did something strange. He took a silver bracelet off his arm, held it out to my daddy, and looked at me.

"You don't have to, Tecumseh," Daddy said, "but I understand that it is impolite to refuse gifts. Very well. Rebecca, come accept the bracelet."

17

I got up. I'd rather sow a dozen rows of corn than go over to the Indian. But we'd all been taught to reverence my father. Still, my legs were shaking as I went around the table.

The Indian's smile was kind. Oh, he drew the eye, all right. When you looked at him, you could scarce look away.

He held out the bracelet. "For you, little straw-hair Becca," he said. And he slipped the bracelet on my wrist. "Now we friends. For always. Yes?"

"Yes," I croaked.

"You've been honored, Rebecca," my daddy said. "Tecumseh is a chief. And you're the first in our family ever to receive a gift from a real Indian chief."

"I want a present, too." John slipped off the trestle bench and ran to Tecumseh. The Indian drew the eagle feather from the band on his head.

Wide-eyed, John took it in his chubby hands. "Thank you," he said gravely.

"Well, we've got to see to the stock." James stood up and signaled to the other boys. Though George was the oldest, everyone minded James. At sixteen he was as tall as George, and like Mama he had the appearance of authority.

"Tecumseh." James drew himself up to full height. "Mayhap you'll be here when we get back."

"He'll be here," Daddy said. "I've yet to serve my potato wine."

Tecumseh stayed long past the time when the candles were lighted. The sun disappeared behind the hills. The redness from it turned to pink, then purple, and he still stayed. My brothers came back from their evening chores, and he was sitting in the guest chair. Only he'd moved it into the room where the walls were made of books.

I put Andrew and John to bed upstairs, came back down, and helped Mama clean up the supper things. All the while I heard Tecumseh and Daddy talking.

They spoke of religion. Of land. Of treaties.

Daddy told him how he'd been here in 1782 with General George Rogers Clark. Tecumseh said yes, Chief Black Hoof had burned the town that was here then. Before the white man could take it. "I no more call Black Hoof chief," he said.

"Is Black Hoof dead?" Daddy asked.

"No dead," he returned. "Chief of some Shawnee. For others Tecumseh is chief."

"Oh," Daddy said.

The boys came back and quietly sat to listen. Daddy told Tecumseh how his father had been a chief of sorts once, too. "A speaker of the Pennsylvania Assembly."

"Make big talk," Tecumseh said.

"Yes, very big talk," Daddy agreed.

They talked about beliefs. Tecumseh told how his people believed that all animals, even the small and weak, have strong spirits. He told how the Shawnees had been on this continent since a thousand years after the Jesus God was born.

Daddy told him how the Galloways had come from Scotland. "During the persecutions of Christians they emigrated across the Irish Sea to Ireland," he said.

"What is this persecution?" Tecumseh asked.

Daddy thought for a minute. Then he said, "Burning."

This Tecumseh understood. He had been a young boy, he said, when he had seen his people torture and burn a white man. "Tecumseh did not speak up and stop this," he said. "But Tecumseh make promise to himself, to never take part in such torture again. And now, the people who call me chief do not do this torture, too."

Pipes were smoked. I felt myself getting sleepy. I thought I would like a game of chess with George. But that would have been rude. My brothers, worn down from the day's labors, lolled about on the floor in front of the big hearth. Mama brought in her mending.

I dozed, leaning against George. In my half-sleep I heard the deep, sure voice of the Indian mixed with that of my daddy's.

Then, of a sudden, everyone stirred. I opened my eyes. The Indian was on his feet. "Must go."

"It's a long way," Daddy said, "and there's no moon tonight."

"Horse by river," he said.

James immediately went to fetch some oats for his horse. Out into the night they went, the two of them, James and Tecumseh.

Before he left, though, Tecumseh bade each of us good-bye. When my turn came, he put his hand on my head. "Remember, little straw-hair girl. We friends," he said.

"Good-bye, Tecumtha."

"I will be back," he said. "By then you have again your teeth. But always you will say my name right, yes?"

I said yes. I felt the touch of his hand on my head long after he left. And the feeling was comforting. I knew it shouldn't be, but it was. And it confused me.

CHAPTER 3

The next day I helped Mama with the laundry. All morning we boiled and stirred, wrung out, and placed shirts, chemises, sheets, and baby clothes on bushes and flat places on the summer grass.

"Why are you getting out the baby clothes?" I asked.

"To see what I have and what I need to stitch this winter."

"Did I wear some of these things?"

"Yes. And John and Andrew after you. We'll need new."

"Do you think it will be a girl?"

"It will be what serves the Lord's purposes."

Did it serve His purposes, then, that I have six

brothers? To what end? Sometimes I wondered about God. Did it serve His purposes that Mrs. Maxwell's only child be killed by Indians?

I kept my ponderings to myself. Though still young, I knew Mama and I were of different minds about things. It was commencing to trouble me. I could never be like her. I liked to question things. She never did.

Laundry is an onerous business but less onerous than soap making or hog slaughtering. And I liked working with Mama. When we were alone together she would tell me things she didn't talk about when the boys were around.

There were things I needed to know. Beside which, I sensed there were things she needed to talk about. She started out all hard and proper with me, but after a while she softened and I got to see a part of her the boys never did.

"In Kentucky you had people to do this for you," I said.

"Yes."

"Then why did you come here where you have to do for yourself?"

"You know why, Becca. We left because of slavery. Your father and I couldn't countenance it."

"But you work so hard now."

"There's times you have to pay for your principles."

If she started on principles, it would have ruined the morning. I cast an eye to where John and Andrew

23

were playing. Near the barn with a cart George had made for them. Then I gave the conversation a different turn. "Why is your name Rebecca Junkin and Daddy's mother named Rebecca Junkin, too?"

"Your father's mother and I are distantly related. We all come from Galloway District in County Antrim, Ireland."

"So, then, I'm part Irish."

"No, we're Scotch." She sighed. "Which is why your brothers are all so pig-headed."

"Couldn't I be just a little Irish?"

"Now why would you want to do that?"

"Irish girls are the prettiest. George said so."

"No need for you to worry on that score, Rebecca."

"But you could say we're part Irish and it would be true."

"We're American, Rebecca. Your father fought for this country in a most perilous way. It's ours, every rock and stream of it."

If she had started on what Daddy did in the war it would have ruined the morning, too. "Do you know that Will is sweet on Elizabeth Pomeroy?"

"Yes."

"She's bound to Owen Davis who owns the mill."

"She'll be free someday. And Will can wait. He's only thirteen."

"She's poor."

"Owen has no children. He'll dower her."

"When I marry, I won't be poor. I'll have silks and a fine house. And someone to do the washing for me."

"He that waits upon fortune is never sure of dinner, Becca."

If she had started with Benjamin Franklin I would have rolled on the ground and frothed at the mouth. "Can I ride over to Mrs. Maxwell's this afternoon? She has a copy of *The Vicar of Wakefield*."

"Yes. I'll be wanting you to take some of the jelly we made last week in return. But be back before the men-folk."

Visiting Mrs. Maxwell was one of my favorite things to do. Because I had no friends my age, Mama allowed it. Also, I think, because Mrs. Maxwell was quality. She grew flowers. She had a pianoforte. Her husband carted it across the mountains the way my daddy carted his books. Mama said you could tell who was quality by what they took pains to cart over the mountains.

Mrs. Maxwell's husband started the first newspaper in the Northwest Territory. There was learning in their house. And no school in Chillicothe. Though there was rumor that soon there would be. If it came, I had decided I would not go. Mama taught me all I should know. Mrs. Maxwell, all the things I shouldn't.

Of course, Mrs. Maxwell was considered by some to be addled. James, for instance. He didn't like that I went there. And was quick to tell Mama and Daddy that Mrs. Maxwell was addled. Thank heaven, they did not listen to his ravings.

I took Oriole. She was old and somewhat addled, too. But we understood each other. Riding her, I could daydream and not worry. She knew the way.

I pondered why James didn't like Mrs. Maxwell. All he could speak against her was that her husband's property lines were sloppy. Sloppy boundary lines were a sin to James, whose dream was to become a surveyor for the Virginia Military District. And William Maxwell had mistakenly built their house half a mile from the property he purchased.

But it was Mrs. Maxwell herself that James feared. She lived in her own place inside her head, and it had naught to do with the lines anybody made on paper for the rest of us. It was why I liked her.

I stopped at the creek to pick some violets for her. When I got to the Maxwell improvement I found Mrs. Maxwell tending her roses. Her husband brought them, too, across the mountains. She had three different kinds and spoke of them as if they were her children.

She also served me tea from China. And cake, soft and spongy. Of course, I told her about last night and Tecumseh.

"He'll be back," she warned. We were in her house. She was brewing tea and setting my violets in a bowl

26

of water. "Indians always come back. Only next time he comes it will be with a band of warriors."

Her face got tight, the way it got when she spoke of Indians. Usually it was open and soft. And friendly enough so you didn't mind the addled look in her eyes.

"He was gentle," I said. "And he gave me this." I showed her the silver bracelet.

She admired it. "Do you know what he was doing the year you were born?"

I said no.

"He was twenty-three years old then. With a party of eight warriors, he scouted around the outskirts of Cincinnati. He put on regular clothing that he'd gotten in raids on white people. He put his long hair under his hat and would walk the streets of Cincinnati. He spoke some English then, too. He would nod politely and say hello."

She was standing, slim and straight, before me. Her jaw tightened, and she looked across the room as if seeing Tecumseh there. "Four times he walked into the fort, watched the soldiers drilling, languished about. Eavesdropped, gathered information. Then he would go back to his friends in camp and a runner would take the information back to Blue Jacket. He learned that General St. Clair hoped to have three thousand troops ready to march in autumn. He learned that half the troops had not arrived yet and supplies were delayed. Finally, when St. Clair and his troops did leave, Tecumseh cheered them on with the other citizens, all the while counting their number. And their guns. Then he rode off on his great black horse to carry the news to others."

I believed her. She knew everything. Her husband made up a book of codes. They had been approved as laws for our territory.

"He'll be back," she said again of Tecumseh. "Likely he's counting the farms around here. And the men. He got in your house like he got in that fort. He'll be back."

I nodded and shivered and drank my tea.

"I must look in my husband's book and see what rules he made for Indians."

Her husband's book was called *Maxwell's Code*, and people hereabouts considered it second only to the Bible. She got a copy down from a shelf, set it on a table, and set more cake and tea out before me.

I stared at the book. We had a copy at home. It came dear. Eighty-six cents a copy. From it my brother George learned how you must turn in the ears and tongues of wolves and wildcats for the bounty. Its laws had to do with everything — the rules for marriage, public whippings, roads, and the safekeeping of prisoners.

I wondered why a man should concern himself with the rules of marriage and prisoners at the same time. And then I minded how Mama worked. And I understood.

I wondered how a woman who lived in her own place inside her head could be so proud of a husband who made the rules for the rest of us. And I did not understand.

"Now!" She beamed across the table at me. "I have news."

This was the moment I waited for. She always had news. "Tell me."

"Edmund Freeman is bringing the *Centinel* from Cincinnati to Chillicothe. He will publish it here!"

"Truly?" Her husband had sold the paper to Freeman two years ago.

"Yes. We will be first now to see this paper that my husband started five years ago. Oh, how I miss it! I stood by my William's side when he wrote and printed it. Did I tell you how he brought that Franklin-Ramage hand press overland from New Jersey to Fort Pitt? And then by boat to Cincinnati?"

"Yes, you told me."

"Edmund is changing the name to *Freeman's Journal*." She sighed. "But it doesn't matter. What does matter is that we'll have a paper right here in Chillicothe. Your brother James must write for it."

I blinked. "James?"

"He writes those marvelous essays. Will you tell him? I've promised Edmund I would seek out James for him."

She admired James. All the women did. They spoke of his sharp mind. But I think his looks didn't escape them, either. I felt guilty, minding how he spoke of Mrs. Maxwell. "James is busy," I said. "He farms."

"Nonsense. Everyone farms. Just like everyone breathes. But we all do other things. I grow roses. Your mama plays the violin. James writes essays."

"What do I do?" I asked.

"What do you want to do, Rebecca?"

"I like to read. I think I might write someday."

"Like James!"

No, not like James, I minded. Never like James. All James wanted to write about was boundary lines and tax laws. "I like poetry," I said. "I like Mr. Shakespeare's sonnets."

"But think! By the time you're grown, *women* may be writing for newspapers."

I blinked again. "Women?"

"And why not?"

I could think of no reason why not. Not here, in this house, across the table from this woman who had put the hot lead in the bullet molds and kept the bullets coming while the men died, screaming all around her, in Virginia.

"You must prepare yourself, Rebecca," she was saying to me. "Women have always done important things. Your father fought in the war. Did he ever tell you why Sir William Howe never caught Washington, pursuing him across the Jerseys?"

"No."

"Being a man, he wouldn't. But I will. Howe had a mistress. She kept him busy. He was always late getting out of bed. This allowed Washington to constantly slip away. We could owe our freedom to that woman. They should make a monument to her someday. Mayhap they will."

Then it was time to go. She gave me the latest copy of the *Centinel*, kissed me, and said come again soon.

I would. There was much to learn.

CHAPTER 4

Our life was strange, a mixture of civilized and savage. Sometimes I got confused. I felt the pull of the civilized when I left Mrs. Maxwell's house with the taste of tea still in my mouth, and a copy of the *Centinel* and *The Vicar of Wakefield* tied to Oriole's back. Then I came past the Paxson's improvement, where I met Indian Joe. And felt the pull of the savage.

Not that Indian Joe was savage. He was not regarded by citizens of Chillicothe as an Indian to be reckoned with. He was not regarded as an Indian at all. He lived here once with the rest of the Shawnees. Sometime between the years of 1779 and 1794, Virginia and Kentucky pioneers set themselves against the Indians hereabouts and chased them out.

The chasing out was called campaigns. My daddy took part in the campaign of '82. And he'd be the first to tell you that the Indians weren't treated fairlike. He got mooded up thinking on it sometimes.

The Indians had to move to the Auglaize Reservation up north. One didn't move. He just sat down and said he wasn't about to go.

Nobody made him. He was crippled by then, and so he just languished around until he became a fixture hereabouts. Aaron and Hannah Paxson, who lived two miles from us, took him in.

He tanned skins, mostly groundhog skins. And he made baskets. He was hobbling along a path by Ludlow Creek when I met up with him.

"Hello, Joe," I called. He waved. I slipped off Oriole's back so I could walk on the path beside him. "When did you get back?"

He went away every spring. Nobody knew where. Nobody asked. He just took his blanket, buffalo robe, fishing things, bacon, and bread and went. He came back in the fall.

"Two suns ago."

"But it's only August." I looked up into his browned, wrinkled face. "Why are you back so soon?"

"The snows will be high this winter. And soon."

I nodded. "Are you checking your groundhog traps?"

He shook his head and pointed to the bundle of

33

willows under his arm. "Oh, for baskets," I said. "Can I help you set them in the bog?"

He grunted yes. I tied Oriole to a tree. We walked to the bog near the Paxsons' springhouse. I handed the willows to him, and he placed them in the bog. When they were nicely soaked, he'd come back, strip the bark from them, and use the strips to weave baskets.

My mama had one of his baskets. Almost every lady in Chillicothe did. Mama's was dainty and held her precious colored threads she used for crewel.

We worked in silence. All around, frogs croaked, insects droned, and sun glinted on the water in the bog. Hard to think that the snow would be high this winter. And soon. I must tell Daddy.

When we were finished, Indian Joe stood up, pointed to my two missing teeth in front, and smiled. "Time to make you a basket."

"What would I do with it, Joe?"

"You grow tall. Be lady soon."

"Never!" I grimaced.

He laughed. Then frowned. "You smart." He pointed his finger to his temple. "Think much. Old enough now to help Indian Joe, eh?"

"Yes, but how?"

"When I die, no coffin."

The sun disappeared behind a cloud. I looked up. Of a sudden I could see the trees unleafed, scraping

34

bare branches against a cold sky. I shivered. "You fixing on dying, Joe?"

"No coffin," he said. "Promise."

I nodded gravely. "How then?"

"Wrap Indian Joe in his buffalo robe. Like I sleep by fire in Paxsons' kitchen. Put me in ground."

He never would sleep in a bed. Mrs. Paxson told Mama it wasn't Christian. Mama said no, but it was likely warm on the floor by the fire.

"Promise," he said again.

"I promise. Any special place you want to do this?"

He pointed in the direction of Hickory Point. It was a small grove on the east side of the Paxson farm. "Old Baldy," he said.

Of course! How stupid of me! Old Baldy was the largest chinkapin tree around. He wouldn't leave in the spring until Old Baldy leafed out. Often he sat under it, working his skins.

We smiled at each other. "It's a good place, Joe," I said.

His smile turned into a rapturous beam. "You will tell them?"

"I'll tell them," I said.

I was pretty puffed up with my own importance by the time our place came into view. I'd been commissioned by Mrs. Maxwell to enlist James to write for the *Centinel*, was bringing home a new book, had learned why Sir William Howe never quite caught

Washington while pursuing him across the Jerseys, was the keeper of Indian Joe's burial request, knew the winter snows would be early, and had stopped to pick some joe-pye weeds for Andrew and John to blow bubbles through. At supper they would all have to hear what I had to say.

Then Josh, Harkness Turner's bound boy, came at me.

"Rebecca? Rebecca Galloway?" He came across the gully from the direction of their house. "Hello."

The Turners were up from Virginia last year. She was from old money and did too much talking about the Old Dominion for my liking. He prided himself on his pedigree dogs. My brother Sam's dogs had better scent and more brains.

I turned. "Hello yourself. I'm late." I was. The sun was already dipping behind the trees on the hill. The family would be to supper already.

Josh was panting. "I need to talk to ye pa."

"What for?"

"The Turners are plannin' a trip over the mountains to South Branch. He needs to know the weather into next week."

"Home to Virginia? What's wrong? They can't abide another winter here?"

"He's got business."

"You mean he's off to get new dogs for his pack."

The boy shrugged.

"They still won't be as good as my brother Sam's dogs," I said.

He didn't argue the point. Just trailed after me as I opened the fence gate and went into our barnyard.

James was there, about to throw a saddle on Saxony. He scowled at me. "You were told to be back before supper."

Did I have to answer to him? I did. "I stopped to talk to Indian Joe."

"You mean you dallied at Mrs. Maxwell's while she filled your head with half-wit stories."

For that he would wait a bit before knowing she'd asked after him to write for the *Centinel*.

"Look at you. Muddy skirts and wet moccasins. You'll get an ague."

I looked down. My skirts were muddy, and, yes, my moccasins were wet from the bogs. Why hadn't I noticed? "I didn't know you worried so 'bout me, James."

He stepped forward as I slipped from Oriole's back. It was a menacing movement. He could slap or not. But all he did was take Oriole's reins.

"I can care for my own horse, thank you."

He grabbed my arm and pulled me out of earshot of Josh.

"Get in the house and stop being such a sassy little piece. Mother needs you. Especially now. Don't you care about her at all?"

He grabbed my shoulder and peered down into my face. I saw the appeal in his eyes. "Aren't you old enough to know what's going on?"

So he knows, I thought. And he's worried for her. I felt ashamed. "Yes," I snapped.

"Then act it. She needs a hand. Go on. Or you'll get one from me."

I grabbed the book and newspaper and went, my face flaming. Behind me I heard Josh. "Could I be speakin' to Mr. Galloway, sir?"

It was just the right note. James liked being called sir. He'd like, even better, to be called squire. "What is it you're in need of, Josh?" He was leading the two horses into the barn. He hadn't been going anywhere, but was saddling Saxony to come look for me.

"The weather."

"Sure you can see my pa. Come on in and sit a piece. We've got a hen on the spit."

My daddy had been wounded in '82. A bullet. Not from an Indian. From Simon Girty, an Indian scout, a white man who'd gone over to the Indians and was not worth the name of either side. The bullet had gone through Daddy's shoulder. It was still in his neck. When bad weather is coming it gives him trouble.

Oh Lordy, I thought. Now Josh will get Sam talking about dogs. All we'll hear about is the merits of hounds. And what makes a good leader of the pack.

And Daddy will start talking about how he rode a mile back to camp after Girty shot him, near fainting all the way. Mama will be disappointed because I'm late, but she won't say anything. James will. After supper. He'll tell her I need punishing. And I'll be sent to bed early. No reading with the family. No telling what I'd learned today. Well, they could all wait to hear. My day was ruined.

CHAPTER 5

Spring 1800

At nine years old, I still felt the pull of both the savage and the civilized. And at times each appealed to me.

Mrs. Maxwell was teaching me to play the pianoforte. I had a new short gown of the brightest blue, thanks to Mrs. White. The Whites came from Kentucky last fall. She knew dyeing. But they lived four miles east. I wanted her recipe for blue dye so bad. Mama was about to let me ride and fetch it when James stepped in and said no. There were painter cats in that part of the woods. So Will went.

He got the recipe for dye. And a bear. Seems the bear was fussing with a painter cat in the woods and decided, right off, that Will looked more interesting than that old tawny cat. Will had to run for the nearest tree. The bear ran round and round that tree, tearing the bark off. Will fired eleven times before felling the beast. By that time James had heard the firing and started off to find Will. But the bear was already dead and Will safe.

We were all proud of Will. But it gave James a turn that his little brother didn't need his help. So he convinced Mama and Daddy I shouldn't be allowed to ride off alone for a while. And I couldn't.

But it convinced everyone, too, that soon I should learn to shoot a musket. George said he'd teach me. Mama never wanted her girl to have to learn to shoot a gun, she said. And she said it with a fair amount of sadness. But I thought it was exciting. What I really wanted was to go on a fire hunt with George.

The newly-named *Freeman's Journal* came to Chillicothe. Mama had a baby girl, name of Ann, but we still had no preacher to sprinkle her. Or Andrew, who was four then and had never been sprinkled or prayed over. I couldn't see how it made any difference. But Mama said it did, that their souls had to be rescued from the grip of Satan. I knew lots of people who'd been sprinkled by a preacher, and Satan had a grip on their souls.

Me, for instance. Times I got so ornery, so plagued

41

with minding the little ones, and seeing Mama work so and wishing for colored cloth, and loving Mama because she was so good and patient, and hating her at the same time because I would never be like her and didn't want to be, that I knew Satan had me in his grip.

I'd grown two inches. James wrote for the paper under the name of Pioneer Junior. I asked Mama why he didn't just write under his own name, but she said it's the way of things for people to have a pseudonym. Look at Benjamin Franklin, he called himself Poor Richard.

I think it's like you're hiding behind a bush. Although I always did think James ought to hide behind something. And I hated the name he picked.

Why a grown man would call himself junior anything is not given to me to understand. If I were writing, my pseudonym would be Daring Nan. Or Wise Wilhelmina. Or She-Who-Won't-Be-Trifled-With. I know, it sounds Indian, but Indian names make so much more sense than ours. And that's what I mean. In so many instances I like the ways of the wilderness better than ours. Then, when we're sitting around the fire at night and the snow is swirling outside and we sing our songs of worship, I know our way is best.

There we were, in a log home in the wilderness.

And oh, it still was wilderness, even though all everybody talked about was how we got three new counties that year and now we can be a state. There we were, singing our hearts out like we used to do in church in Kentucky. And Mama said God heard us.

That was hard for me to believe. I thought God had His mind elsewhere, on Philadelphia, maybe, or New York, where people had all the blue dye they need and didn't need to shoot bears to get it. But when I was singing along with my brothers, who were so tall and strong and could shoot bears from trees, go on fire hunts, and clear stumps from the ground, yet bow their heads in prayer, I felt something rising in me.

Like the smoke from our chimney. Weak against the cold winter sky, yet rising right up to heaven. And I know God must hear us. How could He not? George booms so when he sings.

I got my two new front teeth. And Tecumseh hadn't come back yet. But somebody else came to visit this spring. Blue Jacket. Now, there's a name to be reckoned with.

"Blue Jacket's coming," James said. "I met him in the glen at Yellow Springs. He's on his way here. He's agreed to meet Johnathan Flack at our place in a week."

"What for?" Daddy asked.

43

James had been gone a fortnight, checking faulty boundary lines. He meant to write a report about them. Who read such things? He was full of news. "Blue Jacket said he'd disclose the site of the Shawnee silver mine to Flack."

"Never!" We were at supper. I thought Daddy would choke on his soup. "The Indians will never disclose the site of their silver mine!"

"Blue Jacket says for the right amount of horses, goods, and money, he'll tell," James said.

Daddy's eyes met those of James. And I saw something pass between them. This something passed between them all the time. It plagued the rest of us that we didn't know what it was.

"How many are coming?" Mama asked. And something passed between us in a look. But it was only that I knew she was thinking on how many mouths we'd have to feed. And would the Indians bring women.

"Flack's gone back to Kaintuck to gather a group of backers," James said. "And to get the horses and goods. That's all I know."

The rest of supper was spent conjecturing where the silver mine was.

"Just north of here," George speculated. "Every summer parties of Shawnees come back to Greene County from the Auglaize."

"They also go to Warren County along Caesar Creek," James said.

"Massie's Creek," Will put in. "Right here under our noses. Ezekiel Hopping was captured by Shawnees when they held this land. He told me he and others were marched with blindfolds on, upstream along Massie's Creek, then made to carry heavy sacks back to Chillicothe."

"Wherever it is, they've got a silver mine all right," Daddy said. "Even the poorest Shawnee wears hand-beaten silver armbands. But what's important now is that we've been selected as the meeting ground. It's an honor. They trust us. We're neutral ground. We don't take sides. I don't want any of you badgering the Indians to know about the mine. Not even the lowliest squaw."

"The lowliest squaw won't know English," George reminded him.

"They'll bring interpreters," James said. "They always do."

They did. Her name was Molly Kiser. She was white and the most miserable excuse for a woman I'd ever seen. She wore dirty buckskins and had a tooth missing in front, and she was long past the age where it would grow back. Though up close she didn't appear as old as she did at first.

George said she was only twenty and that she'd

been taken by Indians as a child. And never wanted to go back to her own people, though she'd had the chance.

I saw her in the middle of the encampment, with Wabethe, who was Blue Jacket's wife. The encampment was on our land that ran right down to the river.

They came during the night. I woke up in the morning and they were there. Cooking fires, wigewas, horses, and men all over the place. Then during the morning neighbors came.

Ben Kizer, who spelled his name with a "z" and not an "s" like Molly. Aaron Beall, Adam McPherson, Thomas Townsley, whose Martha was being courted by James. Matthew Quinn, Owen Davis, who owned the mill on Beaver Creek, Solomon McCully, who lived on the north side of the river, Arthur Forbes, David Anderson, and Ezekiel Hopping. James Andrews, who made things out of wood and taught George how. John Nelson, who was a wagoner and once hauled wounded Hessians out of Trenton. Even Colonel Thomas Worthington, whose two-story house had six rooms on each floor and was so fancy they didn't even call it a house. They called it an "elegant seat."

They were all old Revolutionary soldiers. The Virginia Military District was bounty land for men who fought in that war.

"They've all come to get a sniff of where the mine is," George said.

My brothers brought out cider and set a hog on a spit. Mama and I baked the night before. The Indians had their own food but didn't turn away any of ours.

My job, as usual, was to keep the little ones from getting in trouble. Ann was just over a year, running around in a soft little white chemise, barefoot on the grass. I couldn't keep her away from the encampment.

The first afternoon, I walked down there with Daddy and stood around the edges, watching. Flack was bringing forth gifts. Beautiful horses. Copper pots. Muskets. Then came the bolts of colored cloth.

I fair jumped out of my skin, seeing that cloth. What colors! All I could think of was Will having to shoot that bear to get the recipe for my blue.

Blue Jacket sat in front of his wigewa, surrounded by his men. Molly Kiser interpreted. I saw one of Flack's men hold up a bolt of red cloth. Molly fingered it speculatively.

I stood holding a squirming Ann. "What's that Indian going to do with all that pretty cloth?" I asked Daddy.

"He's white."

"White?" I set Ann down. She clung to my skirts.

"He was taken in '71. When he was seventeen. From western Virginia. One day he was out hunting with his brother. They ran into some Indians. He used Shawnee words an old trader taught him. Told them how he'd always admired them and wanted to live their way. Said if they'd spare his little brother he'd go live with them. Turned over his bow and arrow."

Daddy puffed his pipe, watching the goings-on.

"And did he go live with them?"

"From that moment on. Never went back to his people again."

I looked at the man and tried to see the young boy who'd left his family. I couldn't. He looked pure Indian to me. He was confused, I thought, about whether he was civilized or savage. "Why do they call him Blue Jacket?"

"He was wearing a blue linsey shirt when he was taken. His real name was Marmaduke Van Swearingen. He had six white brothers."

Well, if I had a name like Marmaduke I'd rather be called Blue Jacket, too. It gave me no pause that he decided to be savage. Six brothers. Probably all like James.

"He once captured Daniel Boone and my old friend Simon Kenton," Daddy said. "Go fetch your sister."

I looked. Ann was in the middle of the encampment, tugging at Molly Kiser's dirty buckskin skirt. I ran.

By the time I got there, Molly had picked Ann up. I reached for my sister.

Molly smiled. Her eyes were blue, but that was the only way you'd ever know she was white. Her long hair was greasy. She smelled, too.

"Give her to me," I said.

"Pretty baby," Molly said to Ann, who was playing with the woman's bear-claw necklace.

I reached my arms out for Ann. "Give her to me," I said again.

Molly handed her over.

Now I'll have to bathe Ann, I thought. Likely the woman has lice. I ran back to the house with Ann in my arms. Sheriff Maxwell had finally arrived. Daddy wanted him here. There was a rumor Flack had brought liquor. If the Indians started drinking everything could turn bad.

Nancy hadn't come. She was feeling poorly, Sheriff Maxwell said. But I knew better. Nancy Maxwell would sooner stand within aim of a Kentucky rifleman than anywhere near an Indian. Some other women were helping Mama in the kitchen.

Far into the night I heard them out there whooping it up. All afternoon the Indians had played games, run footraces, thrown tomahawks. My brothers were right out there with them, too.

"Blue Jacket's demands are rising," James told us at breakfast the next morning.

On the afternoon of the second day, I wandered out with Ann in tow. The negotiations looked to be getting serious. I saw the men all squatting around smoking pipes. Molly Kiser was smoking, too.

Ann wanted to see the wigewas, so I took her inside one. Here I found sleeping racks. Short, forked sticks were stuck into the ground. Long poles resting in the forks made a frame for the boughs that were covered with soft skins.

Baskets were tied to the inside frame. Some on the floor were filled with cattail fluff. Ann picked some up, delighted with it.

"They use that for stuffing moccasins. Just like we do," I told her.

There were so many things to look at inside the wigewa. Painted gourds, clay pots. There was a big painted rawhide trunk. And deerskins with the hair still on them. Bundles of herbs made the place smell sweet. A fire pit was in the middle of the spotless floor.

I looked around. It was a world of its own. Could I live in one of these, I asked myself? Did Molly Kiser?

Then, of a sudden I heard Daddy's voice in my head. "Fetch your sister."

I looked around. Ann was gone.

Frantically, I searched. I ran outside, looked in

other wigewas, under trestle tables, bushes, blankets, in barrels. Ann liked to hide. And she was so small. Within a few minutes, without attracting attention, I'd searched everywhere. No Ann.

My heart pounded. My mouth went dry. Then it came to me. Molly Kiser had her. I looked. Molly was no longer in the group of men. They were managing without her.

I saw Molly. Down the slope by the river. She had Ann in her arms. How dare she! Ann wasn't allowed by the river!

I ran down the slope. Before I got there I saw that Ann was dripping wet, hair plastered against her face, her chemise clinging to her. She was crying and choking all at the same time. I reached out. "Give her to me! What happened?"

"She'll keep," Molly said. "I got her just in time."

I snatched my sister from her. "What did you do to her?"

"She went to the edge and slipped. I was walkin' to git away from all that men talk. Lucky thing. I fished her out just in time."

"She never! I just turned my back for a minute."

"It's the way of them little ones. S'all right, baby." Molly smoothed Ann's wet hair off her face. "You go back to your playin' now. You just took it in your head to go fishin'. Go on with your sister, honey."

Ann's small hand was clutching Molly's bear-claw necklace. Molly took it off and gave it to her. Ann stopped crying.

I stared at the woman. Was she right in the head? Was I? My sister had near drowned! All because I'd stopped to inspect a wigewa! I started to tremble. Tears filled my eyes as I looked into Molly's flat face with the watery blue eyes, saw the long greasy, lice-ridden hair, smelled the awfulness of her. Bear grease, they use, George had once told me. How could a white woman allow herself to come to such a state?

But she had saved my sister!

How could that be? I read books. All the heroines had long, shining, perfumed hair, gossamerlike clothing. They were delicate and of quality stuff.

"Best take her and git her in dry things," she advised. "She'll be arright. Little 'uns like that kin take it."

I nodded mutely and started up the slope.

"Heard your daddy say your mama's lyin' down. He's busy with the men. No need fer anybody to know. Take her inside and fix her up. I won't tell."

I ran my tongue along my lips, not quite believing what I was hearing. I had done a terrible thing that would surely earn me punishment. And she would keep my deed from everyone.

"Why?" I asked.

She shrugged. "Yer such a pretty little thing. I wuz pretty like you oncet. I'd like to think of ye as a friend.

52

That Wabethe, she's highfalutin jus' cause she's Blue Jacket's wife. Kin I think of ye that way? As a friend?"

I hesitated.

"Friends tell secrets. Kin I tell you a secret?"

I sensed something important coming. "Yes."

"Blue Jacket ain't never gonna tell that Flack where the mine is. It's all a big joke. Indians love their jokes. Gonna lead him on a wild goose chase." She smiled at me with her missing tooth.

I gasped.

"You cain't tell now, 'member. 'Cause we's friends. And that's what friends do. Share secrets."

No, I couldn't. Else my family would want to know how I came by the secret. I nodded. She had saved Ann's life. If I could thank her by letting her think we were friends, it was a small price.

I took Ann in the house. Molly was right. Mama was lying down, sleeping. I changed Ann, put her down for a nap.

Flack and the Indians left on the night of the second day.

"Kaintuck," Daddy told us at supper. "Blue Jacket told them the silver mine is in Kaintuck."

"Never," George said.

Will nodded. "Kaintuck. Along the Red River. I heard them talking."

"I wish I could have gone along with them," Sam mumbled.

"They're lying," James put in.

"Well, they'll find out when they all get there, won't they?" Daddy said.

Yes they will, I thought. And I'm the only one here who knows for certain that Flack will never find it, that it's all a big joke.

I held Ann in my lap. She was playing with Molly's bear-claw necklace. Nobody asked how she'd come by it. But she's taken with it. I'll have to watch her. She's pure taken with everything savage.

For once I knew more than everybody at the table. I felt wise beyond my years. And I couldn't tell.

CHAPTER 6

Spring 1801

My brother George whittled a lot. And when he did it around the fire at night, he told stories to me and the little ones. One story he told went like this.

"Six years ago a man named Alexander McKee bent over outside his home near Detroit and his pet deer gored him in his rump. He bled to death. He was an Indian agent.

"McKee was a fighter, too, always on the side of the Indians. But never wounded. The Indians saw that deer following him around like a dog and thought McKee had special protection from Weshemoneto, their God. So when the deer killed McKee they took it as a sign that God was displeased with them. 'Course, they were suffering famine and defeat at the

55

time, so that didn't help any. And they went, in droves, to see General Wayne and sued for peace, and that's how we got the Treaty of Greenville. And peace between the Indians and whites. Because of a deer."

I don't know about that story. George said sometimes his tales need shaping, like the wood he whittles. But I do know this. We got our second visit from Tecumseh because of McKee's death. Six years after, the Indians held a death dance for him near Detroit. Tecumseh was coming home from it when he came to see us.

Why was I so happy to see him? Why was I so pained at having him see me?

Because I was wearing my old linsey dress, my feet were bare and dirty, my hair hung in my eyes, and ashes were smudged on my face. I smelled of tallow, a fancy name for fat left over from winter cooking. You must make soap in spring before the fat goes rancid. Mama and I both looked a sight.

It was the first warm day of March. Daddy and my brothers were planting. John and Andrew had gone along with them. Ann was sleeping. That red-tailed hawk was screeching again.

First we heard a whinny. I looked up. Down the trace he came, leading his fine black horse. Mama recognized him right off. "It's Tecumseh." She stood up, put her hand to her eyes.

He came from the direction of the sun. The sun got in my eyes first. And then he did.

The sun later went down. But he stayed in my eyes, stuck there from that day on. I was ten years old.

"Mrs. Gal-o-weh woman." He stood in front of us. Smoke from the boiling tallow floated in the air. He waved it away.

"Tecumseh, welcome," Mama said. "We're making soap."

"To wash you clean," he said.

"Yes," Mama agreed.

"Now make you dirty." He smiled at me. His teeth were straight and white in his browned face. His eyes were sad and deep and made me feel pain.

But in that moment I cursed my old linsey dress. I knew how to curse. George and Will did it all the time out of earshot of Mama and Daddy. Shame for the way I looked flooded over me. I wanted, suddenly, to be wearing blue silk. Or red calico. I wanted to be taller and prettier. I wanted a waist and a bosom like Mama had. And at the same time I wanted to hide.

"Straw-hair Gal-o-weh girl," he said. "You have back your teeth?"

I smiled to show him.

"You remember how to say my name?"

"Tecumtha."

"You grow like corn."

"They're all growing," Mama told him. "Some like corn, others like weeds. We have a new one you've never seen. She's napping. Rebecca, go in the house and get some cold cider. And check on Ann."

I ran. Ann was still sleeping in the room she shared with me. I tore off my linsey dress and put on a clean chemise, cotton shirt, and short gown. I took the water that was still in the washbasin from this morning and washed my face. I ran a comb through my hair. Downstairs I fetched two cups of cold cider. One for Mama.

"Why, Rebecca, how nice of you," she said. Her eyes went over me. I could tell that the surprise in her voice was not for the cider.

Tecumseh sat and watched while we finished the soap making. At first he seemed shy, but Mama talked to him like she would to James when he came home from one of his boundary-line trips.

"Where have you been, Tecumseh?" she asked.

He shrugged. "Blue Jacket's town on Deer Creek. Amherstburg, near Detroit town. I went to death dance for Alexander McKee."

"We heard about that," Mama mused. "My son George says two hundred Indians went. Now why would you do this for a white man?"

"To honor him. He was a friend to the Indians."

"George said the death dance went on for two days," Mama said. "He read it in the *Cincinnati Journal*. My."

I stole a look at Tecumseh. What was a death dance? I saw his strong shoulders, his long legs, and tried to imagine him dancing and chanting for two days. By firelight, I thought. He would look good dancing by firelight.

"And where else have you been, then, that made you too busy to come and see us?" Mama asked.

"The valley of the Auglaize." He made a sweeping motion. "I travel much. Many places."

"I understand," Mama said. "You have much to do. We keep hearing that you are becoming an important chief, Tecumseh. But now do you think you could just lift this bucket off the fire for me? The soap seems about done."

Now George had told us that Indians don't do women's work. It is considered not manly. Tecumseh looked surprised at first. I was. I wished Mama hadn't asked him. How could she be so stupid?

But he got up to do Mama's bidding. I noticed the muscles in his arms as he lifted the bucket. He was very strong.

Mama acted very stupid all that afternoon, it seemed to me. She went on and on about things a woman should never talk to an important Indian chief about. We sat under the trees, sipping cider. Mama took up some mending. I brought Ann down from her nap and Tecumseh was completely taken with her. And she with him. She climbed all over him. Mama had to scold her and tell her not to be a trial.

Doesn't that beat all? Mama and Ann were pushy and chatty and he thought they were wonderful. I hung back and he scarce looked at me at all.

"And how are your children, Tecumseh?" Mama asked.

He told her. He had two sons, one six summers, one five. His first wife he had sent away from him, because she was a scold and a bad mother. "Second one die," he said.

Well, that gave me a turn. Two wives! Two children!

"And will you wed again?" Mama asked.

I looked to the fields, hoping to see my daddy and brothers coming. Would they never come? Would Mama never keep still?

"My sister, Tecumapese, cares for the children. She says a chief must have a wife. But I think not for a while."

There were silences while he sat on the ground and gazed off into the spring fields. Then Mama would talk again.

"My sons sowed turnip and pea seeds a week ago. Then we got three inches of snow and that interrupted the work. Now that the weather's finally turned, they're planting sweet marjoram, parsley, pepper and sage, cauliflower and pecan, early potatoes, turnips, and cabbage. My husband kept saying it would snow. He felt it in his neck. But the boys wouldn't mind. They went right ahead and sowed those turnip and pea seeds. He's a regular almanac, my husband, the way he can predict the weather."

"What is this almanac?" Tecumseh asked.

"Why it's the *Kentucky Almanac*," Mama said. "My husband reads it all the time. It tells you how to get rid of the Hessian fly, how to shear sheep, and the proper dates to plant different seeds. It tells when there will be great storms, earthquakes, and eclipses."

Now Tecumseh came alert. "Mukutaaweethe Keel-swah?" he asked.

Mama just stared.

"This e-clipse. The black sun. Your almanac can tell when it comes?"

"Well," Mama said, "of course the men who study such things tell the men who make up the almanac."

"How they do this study?"

"Oh, they are very learned men," Mama said. "From back east in the old states."

"You have this almanac?"

"My husband has it with his books. He'll show it to you later." Mama stood up. "Now the men will be in from the fields soon. Will you stay and sup with us, Tecumseh?"

He stood up. "You make much good talk here, Gal-o-weh friends. I put up wigewa."

"Why, certainly!" Mama was flattered. "There's a lovely spot. By the springhouse."

He pointed in the direction of our wheat field, where he'd been gazing all afternoon. "There," he said. "There is where my mother's wigewa was when I was a boy. There I stay."

George told us another story one night around the fire. It went like this.

"Tecumseh did not want the Indians to sign the Greenville Treaty. He could read and knew what was in it. Two thirds of Ohio and a great part of Indiana were going to the Americans after General Wayne won the Battle of Fallen Timbers. And the Shawnees were to be pushed into tiny reservations in northwest Ohio. So Tecumseh and a band of followers camped outside Fort Greenville and begged the tribal chiefs, as they arrived, not to sign. But the chiefs went in to sign, anyway. Tecumseh and his followers then burnt green wood, setting the fire so the smoke would float into the fort and remind his people who they were and that they must not sign."

This story of George's I believed. It needed no shaping. While Mama and I were readying supper, I slipped into Daddy's book room. I knew where the almanacs were. I stood on a bench and got the latest edition down from a shelf.

"Mama, can I show this to Tecumseh?"

She turned from the hearth. "Yes. That's a wonderful idea, Rebecca. But make sure you don't get underfoot. He's setting up his wigewa."

I ran outside, across our barnyard, and into the wheat field. There were things I needed to know. The almanac was an excuse to get him alone. I knew that once my daddy and brothers came home he would be theirs. And I wouldn't be able to get close to him.

"Mr. Tecumtha?"

He had already set the slender poles in the ground for his wigewa right in the middle of the wheat. He was fastening mats made out of cattail reeds over them. I watched in fascination.

"Yes, little straw-hair girl?"

"I thought you covered your wigewas with animal skins."

"Not always. The white man thinks many things of the Indian that are not true."

"Is it true that the deer killed McKee?"

"Who told you this?"

"My brother George. He tells us stories. But he whittles, too. And he says some stories need shaping, like the wood he works with."

"Indian children always believe the stories their elders tell. Many times told, many times shaped," he said.

I nodded and got braver. "Is it true you camped outside Fort Greenville and tried to get the chiefs not to sign the treaty?"

He stopped working and regarded me solemnly. "George tells this, too?"

"Yes."

He nodded. "It is true."

"But the treaty gave us peace."

"Peace at the cost of my people's destruction." It was said in a becalmed way, with no bitterness.

"There is something I don't understand, Mr. Tecumtha."

"Yes, little straw-hair girl."

"You speak bad of the treaty and the white people. Then why do you come here?"

"Some Shemanese are good. I had a vision that told me this."

"Were we in your vision?" George had told me about Indians and visions.

He smiled. "No. But I know Gal-o-weh people are good," he said simply.

"Do you want to see the almanac? I've got the page where it tells about the eclipse."

He stopped working.

He sat on the ground and listened as I read. "The last eclipse occurred in 1778. The next one will occur in 1806. Five years from now."

He nodded solemnly. "What is this occur?"

"Happen."

"You read much good, straw-hair Gal-o-weh girl. I

64

read but not much understand. I would learn better much."

"I can teach you," I said.

He looked at me. In the distance, by the house, I saw Shag rolling in the dust. A squirrel climbed a tree. A hawk circled overhead. I heard Ann's laugh, a cow moo. Everything seemed so much brighter and certain. Then I saw something in his eyes, some wisdom, like my daddy's.

"You would do that, little straw-hair girl?"

"Yes. I've taught Andrew his letters. I'll soon teach Ann. Just like Mama taught me."

"Good, very. Ann is two summers."

"Yes."

"Don't let her play with her fingers."

I stared at him. "Why?"

"The Shawnee believe that our creator is Grandmother Kohkumthena. She keeps all babies with her until people ask for one after they wed. For the first four years, babies can go back to Kohkumthena whenever they wish. Always give them something to play with. Shawnees believe when they play with their fingers, they are counting the days until they can go back to Kohkumthena."

I stood open-mouthed. Ann always has her hands into something, I pondered. Thank heaven. I smiled at him. He smiled back. "I had a brother named

Joseph. He was two years older, but he died of the fever. Do you think he was counting the days when he could go back to Grandmother Kohkumthena?"

"Many little ones do this."

He knew much. But there were some things I needed to know. "Mr. Tecumtha, did you ever spy on St. Clair's army in the fort in Cincinnati?"

"Yes."

"Have you ever smashed a baby against a tree?"

He scowled. "George tells you this story?"

"No," I said, "not George. Someone else. George says some stories need shaping, not lying."

He stayed three days in our wheat field. Mama and Daddy thought it a mortal sweet idea that I teach him some reading. They suggested I start with the Bible.

I rushed through my chores in the mornings. Then, when Ann was put down for her nap, I'd go out to his wigewa.

He liked the story of Moses.

"This great chief," he said, "has power much, to part the waters."

"God parted the waters. Moses just believed. And you must say much power, Mr. Tecumtha. Not power much."

"What is difference in how I say it and how straw-hair girl say it?"

"It's proper how I say it."

"Did Moses chief speak like this?"

"He spoke proper. Yes."

He made a stabbing gesture with his pipe. "This is why waters parted then. Because Chief Moses speak proper to his God?"

I was becoming confused. "No, Tecumtha."

"Why then?"

"Because he believed."

He scowled. "Tecumtha believed the chiefs would not sign the treaty when he spoke to them, but it did not come to be. Did Jesus God speak proper?"

"Yes. He went to the temple and learned much."

"But they kill him, so even."

"Even so," I corrected.

He shrugged. "Come, read more about Chief Moses, straw-hair girl. I learn to speak proper. But I think this Bible book is like brother George's stories. Shaped like wood with each telling, even so."

That last night at supper he told us what had happened with Flack and the silver mine.

"Flack and his men take Blue Jacket and his people to Kain-tuck-ee," he said. "Much feasting all the way. Many more presents given. Once there, Blue Jacket say he must be alone to fast and purify so he can please the Great Spirit and ask permission to tell white man about mine. Then Blue Jacket tell whites he has vision which says yes, he can tell. Only his eyes too dim

67

to see place of silver. He tells Flack he must send for his son, Little Blue Jacket, who has young eyes and can find mine. He and Webethe leave to get son. Blue Jacket asks whites to wait for his return with son."

"Did they wait?" Sam asked.

Tecumseh nodded.

"How long?" Will pushed.

"They wait much long." And Tecumseh's body shook with silent laughter. "Still wait, maybe. Shawnees still laugh around campfires."

"There's a story for you to tell, George," Sam teased.

"Shawnees tell story," Tecumseh said. "For long time."

Everyone laughed. I didn't. I was thinking of Molly Kiser and wondering how she was keeping.

That night after everyone was abed, I crept downstairs for a cup of warm milk for Ann, who was fretful. Daddy, James, and George were in front of the fire in the book room.

"Did you see the look on his face at supper when I told how Thomas Worthington is agent for those who are leasing land?" I heard George say. "And how a man can get land by promising to clear twenty-two acres by summer? And paying a hundred bushels of corn as rent?"

"It was once their land," came Daddy's voice, quiet and sad.

68

"What do you think he's doing at all these council meetings?" George asked. "He's been traveling all over giving speeches."

"I'd admire to know," Daddy answered. "But I won't ask him. When he's ready to tell us, he will."

"Hostile operations," James said. "There's speculation he's organizing the tribes to attack."

"No," George said, "I don't think so."

I felt a shiver of fear. Would Tecumseh be here in our house as a friend if he meant to attack? Nancy Maxwell thought so.

"We must continue to befriend him," Daddy said. "He must see the white men can be lived with in harmony. That we have the same concerns and hopes they have. Right now he still thinks we're the spawn of the Great Serpent, that we crawled from the sea slime onto the shore to take their land."

"When I get to know some men, I'm inclined to agree with him," James put in.

"He's certainly made friends with Rebecca," George noted.

"Children are best at fostering trust," Daddy said. "If he feels right having her teach him, let it be. It'll keep him coming back. We need that. We need to keep track of him."

By the next morning I knew I needed to have him keep coming back, too. I needed to keep track of him. He was going. I went outside early and saw that his wigewa was taken down. Our wheat field was just our wheat field again.

I handed him a sack. Inside I'd placed some corn bread, apples, and beef jerky, the kind James took on trips.

He nodded his thanks. I looked at him, browned and lean, sure of movement, clear of eye. "Mr. Tecumtha, do you think we're the spawn of the Great Serpent? And that we crawled from the sea slime onto the shore to take your land?"

He smiled. "Not you, little straw-hair girl."

"Will you come back and see us again soon?"

My parents and brothers came out the door before he could answer. Daddy gave him a small old Bible. "Come back," he said.

"Straw-hair girl be high as tassels on corn when I next come," he said.

"Don't wait that long," Mama begged.

I watched him ride away. Don't wait that long. I thought Mama's feelings, but I didn't say them.

Oh, he made such a fine figure on his horse! But, I thought, humble enough to submit to teaching by a ten-year-old girl. Even so.

CHAPTER 7

November 1802

I got to go on a fire hunt with George at long last.

What led to it was that Mama and Daddy went to Cincinnati for the convention to lay the ground rules for Ohio becoming a state. They called it a territorial assembly. They had one a while back here in Chillicothe and a fight broke out.

It was over the boundaries for our new state. James got in on the fight, though he wasn't a delegate. Now he was planning to go to Cincinnati. He couldn't wait to write about it for the paper. Likely a fight would break out there, too, I figured, and we'd never become a state. I didn't care overmuch.

"Mrs. Maxwell says when they lay the new ground rules they won't use her husband's code anymore," I said one night at supper. "I don't see why we need to become a state. Things are fine with me just the way they are."

James glared at me. "Don't be selfish, Rebecca. Things will be better for a lot of people."

"Who?" I asked. "If we become a state, they'll have slavery. Mrs. Maxwell said so. Then we'll have to move again."

"We'll not have slavery," James said. "Mrs. Maxwell doesn't know everything. Things will be a lot better for indentured servants, for one. When we're a state, all indentures made outside of Ohio will now be invalid if they last for more than a year."

Will looked up quickly. "Is this true, James?"

"It's one of the things they want in the constitution," James said gently. "Indentures will be forbidden unless they are entered upon by a mature individual in a state of perfect freedom and for a bona fide consideration."

James used fancy language like that all the time. But it made Will happy. He and Elizabeth were both seventeen then, and all he did was moon over her and count the days until her indenture was finished. She had three years yet to go.

Well, Will had a right to be happy. Though I didn't trust what James said about slavery. And that was one of the reasons Mama and Daddy were going. Daddy said he was going to use all his influence with our delegates not to allow it.

John, Andrew, and Ann were to stay with the Maxwells when they went. I was to keep house for George, Will, and Sam.

I was eleven then. I could make johnnycakes, roast a hen on a spit, boil potatoes, make coffee, and fry pork.

Mama said when she was that age her mother let her go and keep house for a week for a family some miles away with twin girls and an aged grandmother.

It's called "following on" what your mama does. Or if you're a boy, what your daddy does. I'd be in charge of the house. I wouldn't work all day like Mama did. I'd get my chores done early and read. Think of it! All those books in Daddy's book room, mine. No Ann to pull at my skirts. No Mama to badger me to fetch cold water in the gourds. No Daddy to tell me not to fidget at evening prayers. Would George make us have evening prayers? Not likely. He'd want to get to work on the new chair he was making for Mama.

The fire hunt was not part of the following on. And if Mama and Daddy had known about it, they wouldn't have left.

Nor would they have left if they'd known two people would be killed in Chillicothe in their absence.

The two people were James Harrod and Waw-wil-a-way.

Harrod was old. My father's age. He'd been a surveyor, a settler, an Indian fighter. He'd helped to open up the land. They found him on a hill above Chillicothe, scalped, shot in the back, all his belongings stolen. Nobody even knew he was in the territory. He was from Kentucky.

Harkness Turner's bound boy came galloping in on Turner's horse to tell us the first night the others were gone. We were at supper.

"People been sayin' the Indians did it." Young Josh stood, bug-eyed and panting, looking down at us as we sat at our table. "Sent to warn ye. Hostilities could be startin' up agin."

"We're at peace with the Indians," George said. "Sit down, Josh, and have some venison stew. Rebecca made it."

"No thank ye. Gotta be ridin' and warn t'others." He walked to the door. "Scalped," he said again. "'Course, I could take a piece of that corn bread with me."

I jumped up and wrapped some corn bread in a piece of cloth.

"Where's the body?" George asked.

"Over to Gowdy's store."

George got up. "I'm riding over there. Sam, Will,

you stay here and keep things tight. Nobody's to go out. I'll be back soon."

'What about the children?" I asked. "Will they be all right at Maxwells'?"

"Sure enough," George said. "She can hold off an Indian attack, can't she?" He winked at me, then sobered. "I'll stop by and see to them on my way home."

More than anyone in the family, George was following on Daddy. But Daddy didn't look to George for things. He looked to James.

I minded how it hurt George sometimes to know this. But he seemed to go all inside himself with the knowing and get strong. In a different way than James was strong. I liked George's strong better.

Will and Sam played chess, and I read while we waited for George to come back. *Arabian Nights*. I'd waited all day to read it. But now the words made no sense on the page. My back hurt from leaning over the pans in the hearth. I'd chopped and stirred that venison stew till it was mortal tasty. I'd cleaned up the supper things, and all I wanted to do was stare into the fire and watch my brothers. The sight of them gave me comfort while the dark closed round us and the wind picked up outside.

I lighted some tallow candles, the ones made with bay myrtle. Because they gave a good scent. I put up more coffee. Shag barked at every sound, and Will took his musket down from the wall. Shadows played across the rooms. The fire crackled. I fell asleep.

I woke to hear George's quiet voice. "Indians didn't do it. They scalp clean. Whoever did this, didn't."

"Who then?" Will asked.

"Sheriff thinks marauding whites. But there's an alarm out anyway. We stay close to home. Nobody goes anywhere without asking me. I stopped at the Maxwell house. The children are fine. Everything's in order."

That's all he could say, except that we should go to bed. I took Shag with me. When I looked downstairs later, George was wrapped up in a buffalo robe on the floor by the hearth. His musket was next to him. Mrs. Maxwell will be sleeping with a musket, too, I thought. Like she did in the fort so long ago in Virginia.

Three days later Harkness Turner's bound boy came riding in again and told us about Waw-wil-a-way.

"Shot in the back. But he put up a fight. Killed a man named Williams and knocked out another. The third got away. Sheriff is lookin' for him," Josh told us.

We stood in our barnyard. "Why would they attack him?" Sam asked. "He was a harmless old coot."

Waw-wil-a-way, a Shawnee, had been a coming-and-going man around Chillicothe for a while now. His wigewa was on the end of town, and I think he was trying to fix himself as part of the place. Like Indian Joe. Only he made no leather, no baskets. He made only friends.

Now he was dead.

"Well, at least people will be convinced now that Indians didn't kill Harrod," George said. "I feel a sight better about that. Rebecca, give Josh some refreshment."

I took Josh inside to warm himself, for the weather threatened snow. I had cider heating in a pot over the hearth. I gave him meat and bread. He ate hungrily.

"Do you know about the new rules they're making in Cincinnati?" I asked. "That when we're a state all indentures made outside Ohio will no longer stand if they're for more than a year?"

"That a fact."

"Yes. My brother James says so. It means you'll be free."

He shrugged. "Much obliged," he said.

"What will you do?" I asked.

He took his time chewing. He gulped cider and wiped his mouth with his shirtsleeve. "Go west," he said.

"We are west."

He shook his head. "There's more. New land openin' up. Untamed. Wild. Wanna see it."

Dear God, I thought, we've just had a man scalped and another shot. Aren't we untamed and wild enough?

I went on the fire hunt because George would not leave me home alone. My brothers had planned it. The time and weather were right. So George said I was to come along.

I rode Oriole. I was fast outgrowing her. George said I walk more erect and ride more gracefully than any other female in all these mountains round about or the continent at large. "But take Oriole tonight," he advised. "We need no high stepper. We need a horse who knows how to be quiet."

Will rode up front with the fire pan. In it were blazing pine knots that cast a bright, flickering, and eerie light all around us in the woods.

George rode next. Then me, then Sam. I looked around me in the thickets, waiting to sight their eyes.

It's the deer's eyes that betray them. They see the firelight and remain rooted to the spot, gazing on it. Their eyes shine in the brilliance, giving them away.

George called it *shining the eyes*.

We rode for a while through the woods, then Will held up a hand and pointed. We drew up our mounts. I looked where Will had pointed. There, in the thicket, was a pair of shining deer eyes gazing at us.

Never had I seen anything so beautiful! They were round and brilliant. They shone so! They were liquid fire, yet mild and trusting. She sat watching us, completely taken with the fire pan.

"Run!" I wanted to shout. "Run! Don't gaze on it. It will be your destruction!"

In that moment George had taken up his musket, aimed, and fired. I heard the terrible report echo through the woods, heard the thud as the musket ball hit something. The deer.

In the next moment, George and Sam were off their horses and seeing to their prey.

I had wanted to go, but I felt faint. I waited, shivering, while they did what they had to do to the deer and brought it back to throw over the rump of George's horse. Then we went on.

Sam got a deer that night, too. And the whole thing was reenacted. Again, I wanted to scream "Run." But I didn't. I had too much respect for my brothers to do that. And we needed deer meat. Winter was coming.

On the way home, I was quiet. George must have sensed something because he told me a story as we rode out of the woods.

"In North Carolina on the eastern slope of the Alleghenies, young Daniel Boone went hunting of a night. Up ahead his companion rode with the fire pan. Young Boone signaled his friend to stop. He had *shined the eyes* of a deer. They stopped, only, hearing the rustling of bushes as Boone got off his horse, the game fled. Boone sensed it was not a deer and followed."

"What was it?" I asked.

He smiled. "It was a lovely girl with hair like flax. Her name was Rebecca, like yours. She became Boone's wife."

"You're making sport," I said.

"I'm not. When people get smitten with love it's because someone's shined their eyes."

"And is it as fatal as it is to the deer?" I asked.

"Sometimes more so," George said. Then we came out of the woods. He dug his heels into his horse's side and galloped across the field. How did he know? Had he shined someone's eyes? Why did I think he was telling me more than a story?

CHAPTER 8

Spring 1803

I was going to have a fight with James. I just knew it. It had been coming on for a long time, like a case of the ague. We were both burning with the fever of it. And the cause of it all was school.

He had been courting Martha Townsley. Like all soldiers from the Revolution, Mr. Townsley didn't shilly-shally about things.

He wanted to start a school. He'd been scouting up what he needed for it. Support and pupils. He had the support from just about everyone. All he needed was the pupils, enough to make the project worthwhile.

James wanted me to be one of those pupils. I said no. I was twelve. They'll all be ten years or younger. Why should I go? I'd read *Pilgrim's Progress*. I knew the

Book of Common Prayer. I was teaching John to read *Robinson Crusoe*, and he was only nine. I'd taught Andrew his sums and Ann her alphabet. I'd mastered *Dilworth's Arithmetic* and was working on *The History of Charles XII of Sweden*.

That winter I mastered "Chester" on Mrs. Maxwell's pianoforte. It's a hymn from the Revolution. She invited Mama and Daddy to sup and hear me play. She had onion soup, gingerbread, and cake with lemon in it.

Daddy got tears in his eyes when I played. Though I mind that any song from the war would do that to him. Or mayhap it was the onion soup.

Then afterward, on the way home in the wagon when they thought I was asleep, they spoke of school.

"She's right smart, our daughter," Daddy said.

"But I can't send her to school with children," Mama answered. "She's teaching our little ones. It will mortify her."

"Then why not send her to the School for Young Ladies in Cincinnati," Daddy suggested.

Mama didn't answer right off. I laid in back of the wagon, holding my breath. Daddy's words burst over me, just like the northern lights in the dark sky above. Tecumseh told me the Shawnees called them Dancing Ghosts.

"They teach elocution, mantua making, embroidery, drawing, and painting in Cincinnati," Daddy pushed. And his words were, for the moment, like dancing ghosts.

Away? To school? Mama couldn't answer.

Then she quoted Benjamin Franklin, like she always did when she was at a loss for words: "Tim was so learned that he could name a horse in nine languages. So ignorant that he bought a cow to ride on."

"All right," Daddy said. "I know she can learn more from you and Mrs. Maxwell than in any fancy school. And I know you don't want to send her away."

And they spoke no more of it. Until James started in about Mr. Townsley.

I would have died first before I went to school with John and Andrew and Ann just because Mr. Townsley needed pupils and James was courting his daughter. I would perish.

There was much to be happy about that spring. The creeks ran full. The dogwood looked like snow on the hills. And though people never did get themselves convinced that Indians didn't kill Harrod, nobody fired off a musket to mistakenly kill a neighbor. I had a new dress made of the calico that Mama and Daddy brought back from Cincinnati.

We had many new lambs out in the pasture. We became a state in March, and we didn't have to move away. They said no to slavery. And Chillicothe was the capital.

I was going to teach Ann to shell peas. I never did forget what Tecumseh told me about keeping her fingers busy. Besides, she was four and willful. Everyone spoiled her. James always had her on his knee, and he never scolded. George made a cradle for her cornhusk dolls. She was always running to Will saying, "Up, up." And he carried her on his shoulders.

I hated that I was jealous of Ann. I hated, even more, that I was no longer a little girl. In my mirror, I could see I was over-tall. I bumped into things. James said I was clumsy.

I got a bosom then, too. George teased me about it. All the men boasted about having the fastest horse, the best rifle, the ugliest dog, and the prettiest sister. "I've got the best rifle and the fastest horse," he said. "We all know Shag is the ugliest dog. And I'm soon to have the prettiest sister."

I didn't want to be a woman. Some girls couldn't wait. Elizabeth Pomeroy had been ready to wed Will since she was thirteen. What would I do married? Who was around that I could care for? Aaron Beall? He was six feet tall and straight as an Indian, but all he wanted to do was fight. Told George that he hadn't had a fight in a month and if he didn't soon have one he'd have to be "kivered" in salt to keep from spoiling.

That spring the sun poured like warm honey over the hills. The rose cuttings from Mrs. Maxwell that I planted two years ago would soon be in bloom at the edge of the kitchen garden.

The first thing the Ohio General Assembly did when we became a state was make eight new counties. Where we live is Greene County. We have our own courthouse. George helped build it. And that day we were off to celebrate our first court day.

Daddy wrote a note to Governor Tiffin, who lived in a fine house right outside town, asking for some kind of help to quell the fear of Harrod's killing. He said we can't live in fear.

Mama said the day's celebration ought to help. There would be fiddle playing, dancing, good food, and footraces. Unfortunately, there would also be Mr. Townsley. He'd chuck me under the chin and say what a pretty little girl and won't I be proud to have you in my school. And I'd say something vile and disgrace everyone.

I was miserable. I wanted to stay home and die.

Chillicothe had a new inn that year. The Red Lion. It boasted twelve rooms, good clean beds, a constant supply of the best liquor, and room for thirty horses in the stable. But everyone was prouder of the courthouse made of logs.

Our town was only one-half mile long. Besides the inn, there was the land office, the post office, Gowdy's

Mercantile, the *Freeman's Journal* office, and the sheriff's office. Some people who passed through said it was a tolerable bore. James said what saved it was that Massie's Creek not only passed right by, it merged at Chillicothe with the Little Miami River. So we had a small wharf where flatboats or boats of four-feet draft could come. I liked the wharf, but I didn't think Chillicothe was a bore and I didn't think it needed saving.

Everyone crowded around the front of our new log courthouse to greet Benjamin Whiteman, the judge, then rushed inside where it smelled of new wood.

"It looks like a church," Mama whispered. "And if we can have such a fine courthouse, why can't we have a church?"

"Because we have no preacher," Daddy reminded her.

I sat on the log-hewn benches with Mama and Daddy, Ann, John, and Andrew. Up ahead I could see the rest of my brothers.

In plain sight, Elizabeth Pomeroy was holding Will's hand. Well, at least she was honest about being smitten. Martha Townsley held herself apart from James in company, and the other night when she was over for supper they walked out. I wasn't spying, mind you, but I went out to the privy and saw them behind the silver maple tree, and he had his hand on her bosom.

George was standing at the side door, greeting people like he owned the place. Right in front of me, Sam was huddled on the bench with Harkness Turner's bound boy.

"All the way across the country," Josh was saying. "President Jefferson ordered it. Doesn't it beat all?"

"I'd give my lead dog to go," Sam said morosely.

"They follow the waters," Josh said. "The Missouri and Columbia rivers. All the way to the end of the country."

"My lead dog," Sam said again.

"They'll be needin' men. To help. I'm goin'."

"You're not," Sam all but gasped.

"Leavin' tonight. Not waitin' for Turner to come through with my papers sayin' my indenture is up."

"Don't you want to make it legal-like?" Sam asked.

"Don't much care," Josh said. "Those things take forever. Wanna go with me?"

My heart caught in my throat. I looked at Mama and Daddy. Daddy was telling Mrs. Maxwell about his note to the governor.

Then Judge Whiteman took his place at the bench, and everyone stood up. "Good citizens, we thank you for coming," he said, "but there are no cases on the docket to be tried."

A murmur of disappointment went through the crowd. Then the judge held up his hand. "There is, however, a barrel of good Monongahela whiskey at the Red Lion for the celebration."

I helped Mama and the other ladies set out food on the trestle tables on the town square. Everyone ate, and there was much good feeling all around.

But I kept my eyes on Sam. He was huddled with Harkness Turner's bound boy by the water trough in front of Gowdy's Mercantile. The store was open since Mr. Gowdy was not one to pass up opportunity.

I told Mama I wanted to look at the velvet-thick corduroy he carried.

I passed by Sam and Josh slowly. Slow enough to hear Sam tell Josh he'd meet him by Old Baldy, Indian Joe's favorite tree over to the Paxsons' place.

"Eight o'clock," Sam said. "My chores'll be finished. It's the time I go out to see to the dogs for the night."

My heart thudded as I walked into Gowdy's Mercantile. *My brother Sam is running off to go with Lewis and Clark.* And I was the only one to know! What should I do?

I loved Gowdy's Mercantile. I loved looking at the rows of glassware, the jars of pickled and spiced oysters, mackerel, and herring. Mr. Gowdy had barrels of sugar, chocolate, and raisins. The place smelled of chewing tobacco and new leather saddles. Then there were the barter items, things he took in exchange: butter, cheese, eggs, lard, ham, bacon, cabbages, salt, woolen hats, leather deerskins.

Everything was a blur before my eyes. Then the blur turned into James and Martha Townsley at the end of the store. She was holding up some bright calico.

"Rebecca," Martha said, "hello."

I nodded politely.

"Come see if you like this calico."

There was nothing for it. I had to walk over and pretend to look and be taken with the stuff. "It's lovely."

"Do you think it too bold?"

"Not for you," I said.

James leaned against the counter, scowling, trying to decide if I was being sassy.

Martha laughed. "I consider that a compliment. I hear you're going to be one of the first pupils in my father's school, Rebecca. How nice for you."

"It's Mama's one true heartbreak that there isn't a proper school here for you," James said.

"I have been properly schooled. And Mama has other things to break her heart," I said.

"Like what?" James challenged.

I shrugged. "I'm not ignorant."

"James doesn't mean that you're ignorant, Rebecca," Martha put in. "He's as concerned about you as he is about all his brothers and sisters."

I looked at my brother. Is he? I thought. If he were, he'd know what Sam is fixing to do out there by the trough with Josh. And not be in here fussing with her over calico.

If he were, I'd be able to tell him what Sam is fixing to do. And have him stop it. Before Sam becomes Mama's one true heartbreak.

But I did not answer. No sense in baiting James. I couldn't think of the fight over school now. I must think on what to do about Sam.

And then we heard the yell from outside. "I'm gonna beat the livin' hell out of you, you skunkin' liar!"

"Hurrah, Ben, you tell 'em. He's been lookin' for it. You give him what for!"

James pushed past me out the door. We stood on the front porch of Gowdy's Mercantile. A crowd had gathered in the middle of the road in front of the Red Lion. They were yelling and cheering two men, who both had their shirtsleeves rolled up and were circling each other like angry dogs.

"Fight, fight." Some little boys ran past Gowdy's to join the circle.

"Good lord," I heard James say as he started off in the direction of the crowd. "It's Ben Kizer and Aaron Beall. Stay inside with Martha, Rebecca."

I did not stay inside. I followed the others to the edge of the circle. I stood on tiptoe, like the other women were doing, to see what was happening.

First it was only Kizer and Beall, whose face looked reddened by either the May sun or the Monongahela whiskey or both. Beall's eyes were gleaming as he danced around his opponent.

Kizer was yelling that he could whip Beall. Each had his own supporters cheering him on, but Kizer's were the loudest.

"Gouge him!" someone yelled. "Hit him square!"

"Fight fair, gentlemen," shouted Colonel James Collier from his horse.

They started punching then, though it seemed to me there was more dancing than hitting going on. Then Beall attacked, his fists pounding Kizer in the sides. You could hear Kizer's ribs crack.

Kizer's friends rushed in to tear him away from Beall's grip. But two of them got caught by Beall's terrible fists and were knocked down. Then Beall started on Kizer again, pounding with those fists.

"Away, children, away!" Mrs. Maxwell and some of the other ladies, seeing there was going to be a real bloodletting, gathered the children and retreated to the town square. Mama grabbed me, but I pulled free. She had all she could do to manage Ann and Andrew and John.

Of a sudden Sheriff Maxwell came rushing through the crowd with a couple of other men. Two of them were my brothers Will and George. "All right, let's break this up!" Maxwell yelled.

Immediately Beall turned on him and hit him in the eye. I heard the sickening thud, saw Maxwell go down, saw some of Beall's friends take off their hunting shirts and plow into the fray. There was a tangle of

91

arms and legs. Everybody seemed to be in on it. I saw George rolling on the ground with Beall and felt real fear. Sheriff Maxwell was half sitting up on the ground, bleeding from his eye and holding his ribs.

Two men carried him off and put him on a trestle table on the green. Women screamed and ran for water and hovered over him.

George and Will were still fighting and getting the worst of it from Beall and his men. Then Sam came pushing through the crowd and James behind him.

Sam was sixteen and not as strong as Will or George. In a minute James was there, pulling him back. Nobody else paid mind, but I did. I thought James and Sam would start their own fight, but James, being stronger, hustled Sam away.

Will's shirt was torn half off. I heard my father's shout. "Stop it now!" His voice had power and authority, but no one listened.

Kizer was down, but Beall was still pounding him with his fists. George dragged him off and got a back-handed blow from Beall for his trouble. George swayed and hit the ground hard.

Two men carried Kizer away.

"Has he no friends?" Beall roared.

Will stood there, facing Beall, panting and wiping sweat from his eyes.

"No!" I heard Mama's cry from the edge of the crowd.

"I don't wanna kill you, kid," Beall was saying to Will. But Will was advancing on him. For a moment there was dreadful silence. Behind me I heard Mama's low sobs.

Then someone fired a gun and everything stopped. My daddy stepped into the circle, holding his musket in one hand, barrel pointed in the air. "It's over," he said. He looked at Beall, then at Will. Neither of them moved.

George stumbled to his feet, grabbed Will's arm, and pulled him away. Will shoved George aside. He seemed to be in some other place, not hearing.

Elizabeth Pomeroy was next to me then. "Oh, make him stop, Mr. Galloway," she pleaded.

Daddy fired his gun in the air again, and some women screamed. "It's over," Daddy bellowed. "Kizer is near dead."

James stepped into the circle, went to Will, and said something low in his ear. Will shook his head. James grabbed him and pulled. And for once in my life I was glad that James held sway over us younger ones. Will went with him.

They took Kizer home in a wagon. But not before Sheriff Maxwell, limping and holding a rag over his eye, issued some warrants.

Eight cases of assault and battery resulted. The first session of Greene County Court was in session. Judge Whiteman presided that very day.

* * *

We got home late. The cows had to be milked, the stock fed, and the young ones put to bed. After Ann was settled down, I ran out into the sweet May dusk. Sam was feeding the hogs.

"I heard you today. Are you going, then?"

"Going where?"

"I heard you in the courthouse. And by the water trough. You know where. With Josh. To join Lewis and Clark."

He gave a short, bitter laugh. "You read too many books, Rebecca. That imagination of yours needs reining in."

"Don't put me off, Sam. I *heard*."

"So? What do you aim to do about it? Or have you done it already?"

"I haven't snitched on you. I wouldn't. Don't you know me better than that?"

He shrugged. "I gotta help Will and George. They're hurting."

"Sam, don't go, please." I put a hand on his arm.

He looked at my hand, then me. "Do you think anybody would care?"

"Yes. It'd kill Mama. And Daddy."

"He doesn't even know I'm alive. It's all James with him. We know that. At least Will has Elizabeth. And George his woodworking and all the girls he carouses with when he goes off to help build some new court-house."

"George?" I gaped.

He laughed. "Why d'you think he's so anxious to go to Warren County next month? He's got women in every one of the eight new counties they just made."

George. I closed my eyes. No, I mustn't think of that. It's Sam I must think of now. "You've got your dogs. Who will see to them?"

"I'm training up John. He's interested."

"He's only nine."

He grunted.

"I'd die if you ran off, Sam. I truly would. Please don't go."

He grunted again and went back into the barn.

After chores, Daddy called us all into the book room.

George's head was bandaged, his arm in a sling. Will was limping. Daddy was grim.

"Today was a disgrace," he said.

Nobody argued.

"I don't know if my boys were coming to the aid of a whipped man or joining the fight for the blood lust of it, that's what worries me."

Nobody said anything. The clock struck seven. I saw Sam look at it, then me, and drop his eyes. He hadn't fed his dogs yet for helping George and Will.

"We may be a new county," Daddy went on, "with a courthouse and an inn with twelve rooms. We may be the state capital, but today proves that we're still not civilized. We've got ourselves to fear more than the Indians."

Mama nodded. What was coming? Something. I'd seen them conferring in their room when I brought Ann up to bed.

"We're sore in need of spiritual guidance," Daddy went on. "It's about the only thing we don't have out here. James and Martha are fixing to wed. So are Will and Elizabeth. The little ones haven't been sprinkled yet. We need a minister, and I aim to get us one."

We looked at each other and waited.

"Your mother and I have discussed it. James and I leave at the end of the week for Kaintuck. I hoped for us to take a trip there on business this fall, after harvest. But now I've decided that it can't be put off. And that our first business is to secure a preacher to bring back here to Greene County."

James again. I looked at Sam. The look in his eyes said it all. "See?" it said. "Why not me? Why not George or Will?"

"We leave at a bad time," Daddy was saying. "The winter potatoes still need to be planted. There's the mid-June harvest of cucumbers, squash, and peas. A lot of work. We can't make this trip unless I can count on George, Sam, and Will. Or everything will be lost."

Silence. Then George spoke. "I'll do my best, Pa. They can get along without me in Warren County next month."

"No, you go. It's only for a week. It's not you I'm worried about. I can't make this trip at all unless I can depend on Sam and Will. Well, boys?"

But it was Sam he looked at. And it came to me then.

This wasn't about Greene County needing a spiritual adviser. Or anybody about to wed or needing sprinkling.

This was about Sam.

Daddy knew Sam was planning on running off this night. No minister was important enough to leave the farm midsummer.

Daddy was risking the farm to keep Sam.

"We can do it, Pa," Will said.

"Sam?"

My brother raised his eyes. Some spark of defiance had gone out of them. But something came into them now that had never been there before. Some determination.

"Don't worry none, Pa," he said.

"Then we leave at the end of the week," Daddy said.

And so they left and Sam stayed. Though Harkness Turner's bound boy was gone the next morning. Everybody wondered why. If Josh was the running kind, people conjectured, wouldn't he have run *before*? And couldn't he have waited for his papers saying his indenture was over? What was he running *from*? You just couldn't figure young people these days.

Nobody thought to ask what he was running *to*. Only I knew. And Sam. And we weren't telling.

CHAPTER 9

The older I got the more I came to know that there were lots of things Daddy didn't tell us. George said he learned to keep his mouth shut as a soldier.

But the night before he and James left, Daddy told us he'd gotten a note from Governor Tiffin. "In response to a note of mine to him," he said. "I asked him to invite Tecumseh to Chillicothe to calm the people who have fears about Indian attacks."

"Did he?" George asked.

"Yes," Daddy said.

"And?" George pushed. "Is he coming?"

"Yes," Daddy said.

"When?" We all asked at once.

"Soon. Likely while James and I are away."

"What makes you think he can calm people?" Sam wanted to know. "Matt Quinn says the first Indian he sees, he's going to blow his head off."

"That's exactly the kind of thinking we have to guard against," Daddy said. "But in answer to your question, Tecumseh has become a practiced speaker. He's been traveling all over, talking to different tribes. They respect and listen to him. I think our people will not be disappointed."

"What do you want us to do, Pa?" Will asked.

"Welcome him," Daddy said. "Let him pitch his wigewa in the wheat field. And don't ask what he's been about in his travels."

Before they left, James surprised me. He gave me Saxony for my very own.

It was not done without a lecture, of course. When James is nice, self-righteousness is always a part of it. First he preached to the little ones about obeying and helping. And outlined what punishments lay in store for them when he returned, if they made any trouble.

Then he asked me to walk him out to the barn.

I kept my silence, conjuring up the mettle to match wits with him. We walked through the barn to the stall of his new horse, Harmony. She's a pedigree. He purchased her from Thomas Worthington.

"I want you to take care of her for me," he said.

Sam had told me James was taking her to Cincinnati in October for the two-day racing event. Last

100

year the purse was fifty dollars. Horse racing is becoming very popular because the settlers hereabouts come from Kentucky and Virginia.

"I'm not your personal groom, James," I said.

He made like I hadn't sassed him. "You've outgrown Oriole and become a fine horsewoman. I wouldn't trust the others with her. Take care of her, and when I come back I'll give you Saxony."

I gasped. Saxony was no slouch. "Do you mean it?"

"Take care of Harmony. Clean her stall, brush and exercise her every day, and when I come home see if I don't mean it."

"I'll do it," I said.

"Go easy with her. No racing. She goes like the wind. If I hear you raced or come home and find you with a broken leg, the agreement is off. And see that you don't neglect your chores. Mama comes first, remember that."

Saxony for my own! My head swam. Oh, how I hated myself for showing such pleasure. Did I have no backbone at all? I didn't, I decided. Who needed backbone? I was getting Saxony.

I rode Harmony every day. Mostly I rode on the east side of town along the stream we call Oldtown Run, then out onto the prairie that's south of the town.

She had power and grace. When you ride a horse like that you have power and grace, too. And you tend to think more of yourself than you are. No wonder James acted so superior, I thought. He always had the best horses.

I was riding Harmony when Tecumseh came. First I saw the red-tailed hawk, so I wasn't surprised when I saw him in the wheat field, setting up his wigewa. Somehow I already knew that hawk was, in some way, connected to him.

I rode right over to say hello. I knew how I looked riding Harmony. George had told me. "Better'n any girl in the county."

Tecumseh did not know me at first.

"Hello, Mr. Tecumtha."

Then he knew me and smiled. "Straw-hair Gal-o-weh girl."

I saw admiration in his eyes. And surprise. As if it had been longer than two years since we'd last met. And that made me glad.

"You ride like man," he told me.

"I'm the best horsewoman around. Even my brother James says so. This is his horse, Harmony. He's going to run her in Cincinnati in the fall. I can shoot a musket now, too. George taught me."

"You learn much from your brothers."

"Yes." I slipped from Harmony's back. "I can outrun and outleap any female around here. And they're all older than I."

102

He looked grave. "Tecumapese, my sister, cannot ride like this. But I learn much from her."

I became indignant. "Like what?"

"She teach me how everything does not come at once. Sometimes we must wait. Shemanese has word for this."

"Have," I said. "Shemanese have. And the word is patience."

He nodded. "She teach me how to look upon these who are hungry or sick."

"Those," I said, "and the word is pity."

"She teach me to speak truth at all times. And that our most important possession is honor. I listen to Tecumapese though she cannot ride like Gal-o-weh girl. She is *ichquewa*."

"*Ichquewa?*"

"Woman."

I tossed my head. "I don't want to be a woman, Tecumtha. All we do is work and take care of the little ones. My brothers have all the sport."

He turned away from me to tend to his wigewa. "When Shawnee girls become *ichquewa*, these stop playing with their dolls and learn the ways of *ichquewa*."

"They," I said. "And I don't play with dolls."

"You play with horse," he said.

Well, I never! So that's the way it was to be, then.

103

"Just because you've become an important chief invited here by the governor to speak to our people doesn't give you the right to chide me," I said.

"What is this chide?"

"Never mind. I thought we were friends."

"Women are sacred." He went on as if I hadn't spoken. "They are givers of life. They are to be treated with respect. You should not turn away from being woman."

I climbed on Harmony's back. She wanted to run. I reined her in and looked down on him from my perch. I saw that he was strong and beautiful, his teeth so white, his eyes so intelligent, his moves confident. But I was disappointed.

Tears of bitter disappointment crowded my eyes. I'd waited for him to come, and now he was treating me the way James treated me. "You'd best save your speechifying for those who want to hear it," I said. "I'm no silly goose to be taken in by your airs."

"What is this airs?"

"People around here are a feisty lot. You talk to them like that and all you'll do is stir things up." I didn't wait for his reply. I pressed my heels into Harmony's sides and galloped off toward the barn.

He'd come and we'd fought in the first five minutes. What had happened? I watered Harmony, washed my face in the bucket outside the door, and went in to help Mama.

At supper I did not speak to him or look at him. Several times I caught him looking at me and cast my eyes down. Then a sharp pain would go through my middle, like when I've eaten too many huckleberries.

Why did I feel there was going to be trouble? Why didn't anyone feel it but me? I looked at my family. How could they sit and sup, how could George explain so easily to Tecumseh the difference between a territory and a state when all around me I felt the air charged with something I could not name?

My brothers were riding over to the Maxwells later for a meeting of the militia that was to guard Tecumseh tomorrow.

After supper, instead of wanting my help, Mama pulled me aside. "You must ride over to the Maxwells with your brothers. Nancy doesn't want to come to Tecumseh's speech tomorrow."

"I didn't expect she would come, Mama. She hates Indians. She didn't come when Blue Jacket was here, did she?"

"That was different. She can hate them all she wants. Her husband is sheriff. Tecumseh was invited by the governor. It's her bounden duty to come. Only you can persuade her. Go. I can do without you here for an hour or so."

Tecumseh had gone outside. As I walked across the barnyard, he came at me. "We collide like two buffalo," he said.

Well, I couldn't have put it better myself.

"Tecumseh is much sorry he offend friend."

I didn't know what to say to that. James never apologized. I nodded.

We stood awkwardly, looking at one another. From the corner of my eye I saw my brothers leading out the horses, holding the reins, talking, kicking the dirt. But I knew they were waiting.

"Tecumseh does not understand ways of Shemanese yet. What means this feisty lot?"

I smiled. "All the men who have settled in the Virginia Military District are old Revolutionary War soldiers. They're fighters. Harrod was killed, and they're angry. They're not about to be trifled with or have their families threatened. They've heard you've been going around, traveling and giving speeches. They think you're spiriting the Indians up to attack us."

He said nothing.

"My daddy said we're not to ask you why you're meeting with Indians and speechifying so much. But I need to know."

"Why should Tecumseh tell little straw-hair girl?"

"Because you said I'm a woman."

He folded his arms across his middle. Lord, he's

beautiful, I thought. Lord, I must be coming on to be a woman. I never felt so in his presence before.

"Tecumseh has decided not to be a warrior with guns and war clubs," he said. "These are foolish. Tecumseh has decided to be a warrior with words."

"Those are foolish," I corrected. "These is the plural of this. Those is the plural of that."

He shrugged. "Tecumseh has given up the dream of winning the war with the Shemanese. War is foolish whether called this or these. Tecumseh has decided that if all Indians unite like the Shemanese, they will have-has to negotiate with us in an honorable way."

He smiled. And oh, it drew my eye.

"You help Tecumseh with has-have words for speech tomorrow?"

"Yes. I'll be back in an hour. I'll help," I said.

A group of horses were tethered outside Sheriff Maxwell's house. Men lounged about on the porch. Militia. Our neighbors. I was the only female present, and several of the men glanced at me as my brothers walked me to the porch. They know why I'm here, I thought. How awful for Sheriff Maxwell. He's a major in the militia.

Inside, Sheriff Maxwell welcomed me. "Go see her," he said. "Please. She'll listen to you."

He was no major now, no sheriff, but a bewildered

husband whose wife was refusing to do her bounden duty. Her absence tomorrow would be a humiliation to him.

He needed me. I went. I didn't have time to feel important about it. She needed me more, and she was my friend.

I found her in the parlor, sitting primly with a Bible.

"If you've come to persuade me to go to this thing tomorrow, Rebecca, I can't do it."

"I know," I said. I sat down next to her. I took her hand.

She looked at me. There were lines in her face I'd never noticed before. Her hair was streaked with gray. "At night I still hear those Indians attacking the fort at Grave Creek. Did I tell you how I volunteered to go for powder when we ran out?"

"Yes," I said. "But Elizabeth Zane was chosen to go instead."

"Because I was better at molding bullets. The powder was in a cabin outside the fort. They didn't think Elizabeth would make it back, but she did."

"You've told me many times," I said.

"Elizabeth became famous for running for the powder. Wherever they tell tales of Indian attacks, they tell of how she went for that powder. Did I tell you how my baby died?"

"Killed," I said, "in the attack."

"How?"

"A stray arrow."

"No."

"But that's what you said."

"No." She looked down at her Bible. "Do you know what this book says about children?"

"Tell me," I said.

"That they are our true inheritance. That they will grow straight and tall and go to meet the enemy at the gates. Your mama has so many sons, Rebecca. They are all so straight and tall. There are so many to meet the enemy at the gates."

I could not speak.

"And she has you and little Ann. I had just the one son. He was not killed by an arrow. He ran outside. We were busy, fighting. I don't know how he got out. An Indian took him and smashed him against a tree."

I stared at her. The horror of her words washed over me, drowning me. Can words drown you? Hers did. I could scarce breathe.

"So you see why I can't go tomorrow to hear Tecumseh speak, don't you? I have no son to meet the enemy at the gates."

How can I ask her to come? I thought. How can anybody ask her to do anything?

I reached for the right words to say. But there were none. I decided that right off. So I just said what came to my mind.

"I don't want to be a woman," I said. "I don't want to have a bounden duty to any man."

"I know." She smiled at me.

"Tecumseh says women are sacred."

She gave a little snort and shook her head.

"He says they are to be treated with respect. He says his older sister taught him patience and pity and to speak the truth always. And that their most important possession is honor."

"What is honorable about smashing a baby against a tree?"

"He doesn't do that."

"You *believe* him when he tells you this?"

"Yes."

"How can you?"

I shrugged. "He's different, Mrs. Maxwell. He's trying to teach his people to be different. He's broken away from the other chiefs to make his own way. He has his own following."

"You're teaching him to read."

"Yes."

"How does he seem to you, then?"

"Like he means what he says."

She shook her head. "I know I should be there tomorrow. I know what it will do to my husband's standing if I don't go. How can I go, Rebecca? Tell me."

I took her frail hand in both of mine. "Everyone is afraid," I said. "My daddy asked the governor to send for Tecumseh. To tell us that the Indians aren't going to attack. My daddy believes in Tecumseh, and he fought the Indians, too."

She nodded, but I could tell she still wasn't convinced. I wasn't convinced myself. Oh, I believed in Tecumseh. But I wasn't convinced it was right to ask this dear woman to stand there and listen to him make a speech. And if I'd known before what she'd just told me, I wouldn't have come.

But I'd come. I was here. And she was looking to me for help. Not so much for tomorrow. But for herself, beyond tomorrow.

Then I had a thought. "How old would your son be now?" I asked.

"Twenty-two."

"He'd be tall and straight," I said. "He'd be in the militia, like my brothers. And tomorrow he'd be there. To meet the enemy at the gates."

She nodded, waiting.

I had to clear my throat to go on. "Well, he can't be. So you have to do it for him. You have to stand there, tall and straight, and do it for him. Don't you see?"

She nodded slowly.

"I'll stand with you," I said. "We'll do it together. What was his name?"

"Billy."

"We'll do it together. For Billy. What do you say?"

She closed the Bible in her lap. She put her head in

her hands and wept. Her shoulders shook. I hugged her. Then I went outside to tell Sheriff Maxwell that it was all right. She'd be there tomorrow. He could count on it.

Mama had the bay myrtle candles lighted in the book room when I got back. She was reading to the little ones. No sooner did I come in the door than Tecumseh followed. He stood there, waiting to be invited in.

Mama looked at me. "I've promised to go over some words for his speech tomorrow," I said, remembering. I didn't want to do it. All I could think of was Mrs. Maxwell's baby.

Mama nodded and invited him in.

We sat a long time going over the these-those words. And others. Mama put up coffee. There was fresh corn bread. My brothers came in and sat down listening.

"These people are here with us now," Tecumseh said, repeating the words after me. "They were here yesterday."

"Yes," I said, "and those people are across the room."

"Those people are in my tribe?"

"Yes, but they can be these when in the present tense."

"But I lead them all. These and those."

"Yes. All of them."

He scowled. "Am I these or those?"

"You are one. You are he. Or him."

"He pounded his chest. He. Him. What is this tense?"

"If you've already done something in the past, you have done it. You're speaking of something already done."

"Tomorrow I speak also of what I will do. What these-those words do I use then?"

I looked at my brothers. They smiled.

"Just tell them what's in your heart, Mr. Tecumtha," I said. "They'll understand. And we'll study more on this in the future."

He told them what was in his heart. Five hundred people and the governor came to hear him, from far and wide.

He stood in front of the courthouse. My brother George said he'd gone to the river to bathe early in the morning.

"He's wearing buckskin," George told us at breakfast. "A loose shirt. He said if he were going to battle he would wear nothing loose for the enemy to seize and hold on to. So we're honored. He doesn't consider us the enemy."

Tecumseh spoke for two hours, and the crowd never became unruly, never grumbled, never shouted or showed disrespect. Of course, the militia was there. But I think it was not needed.

He made an imposing figure. Some people gasped just seeing him. And I felt proud.

He's our Tecumseh, I told myself. Our friend.

He told the crowd that his people were abiding by the Greenville Treaty, and they had not killed Harrod. He said that Waw-wil-a-way had been killed by white men, but there was no bitterness. The old man had died a true warrior. There was honor in his death. The Indians did not wish to strike back.

He said the whites and Indians should go about their business. That each had much to do and should not waste time on fear. Or resentment.

I stood beside Mrs. Maxwell. I held her arm and felt the tremors in her body as he spoke. But she stood erect. Her husband stood next to her.

"We must not fear and mistrust each other," Tecumseh finished. "Our sons and daughters must not learn this fear. They must grow tall and straight without it."

Mrs. Maxwell squeezed my hand. I squeezed back.

When it was over, people crowded around him to shake his hand, to pat him on the back, just to get near him. Mrs. Maxwell and I got pushed aside. And I had a terrible thought.

He isn't our Tecumseh, I minded. He's a powerful speaker. Like my grandfather was in the Pennsylvania

Assembly. He's a leader. He's going to travel far to do this speaking, and people are going to look for him. Soon he'll belong to many others.

I was going to lose him as a friend.

I felt mortal sad. If I were an Indian I suppose you could say I'd had a vision.

CHAPTER 10

October 1803

Daddy and James were coming home. The mail coach brought a letter. They will be home any day now.

Mama went around the house singing. She said we must clean the house from top to bottom.

They were bringing a minister. His name was Robert Armstrong. His wife's name was Nancy.

Best of all, this Nancy was bringing with her a young sister. My age! Her name was, of all things, Euphemia, but they called her Phemy. They would stay with us a few days, then with the Maxwells until they got settled.

Oh, I was feverish with waiting! To think, a girl my age was coming to visit! What would she look like? Would she have curls? Calico dresses? Would we be able to lie in bed at night and whisper secrets before we went to sleep?

I cleaned my room. I gave my bed to Phemy. I put my good quilt on it. I slept on a cornhusk mattress on the floor. Daddy and Mama gave their room to the minister and Nancy and put up a blanket partition over the book room and slept there.

Mama and I got out the good carpet with the flowers on it. And the branch candlesticks. I picked wild grapes and some hickory and butternuts and helped Mama bake apple and peach pies from the fruit in our orchard.

I washed the good cups and saucers. "Let me set the board," I begged Mama. "I'll serve dried beef cut in slices, custard pastry, and a dish of nut cakes and sauces."

She smiled. "Very well, but I think we'll also put a ham on the spit and serve some corn, squash, and peas. They'll be hungry."

They were due in a week.

Sam, Will, and George set themselves to cutting the Indian corn before they arrived. The pumpkins lay scattered in the fields. We fed some to the cattle and dried some for our own use. Our orchard trees were heavy with apples. I threw them down to Andrew, Ann, and John, who put them in baskets. Sam took them and our Indian corn to Owen Davis's mill. Davis took a tenth of the lot of corn in payment. And a shilling for every barrel of cider he made. But we didn't mind. Mama said he'd dower Elizabeth well before she and Will marry.

Oh, there was so much work, yet the time passed so slowly! I minded how Tecumseh had told me that the Shawnees believe in the Great Turtle, who carries the world on his back.

Those days, waiting for my father, I believed in that turtle, too. Because the warm October days dragged on. The Great Turtle was crawling, taking his time about things.

And then one fine blue morning I went outside to fetch water and I felt a coolness in the air coming down from the English lakes north of us.

I saw the wind walking through the wheat field. I heard the water in the creek rushing over the stones. I looked up the Bullskin Trace and saw them coming in the distance, three horses, three riders, and a wagon pulled by a team.

I dropped the bucket and ran through our farm yard down to the Bullskin Trace. Shag ran with me and saw them, too, and commenced barking wildly and running in circles. Then Sam's dogs started in their pen.

My daddy was back! News of it went over the hills and ran with the water in the creek. The bullfrogs croaked out the news from their lily pads on pools of water at the edges of the Little Miami River. The

118

wind picked it up and ran through the wheat field with it. My daddy was home, all the way from Kaintuck, over the mountains before the first frost of winter!

Our first meal together then was breakfast. I couldn't serve the custard pastry I'd made. Mama put up a big pot of coffee. Sam went to the springhouse for fish he'd caught in the stream. George got a side of bacon, and I started to fry it. John got fresh eggs from the henhouse. As Mama had said, the travelers were about starved.

After hugs and cries and shy hellos and some tears from Mama, she made ready three measures of fine cornmeal and patted it into cakes that I put on the hearth.

I set the table while my brothers put the saddlebags and bedrolls into the book room and went outside with James to shove each other around and pat each other on the back.

I stole looks at the company. The reverend man was tall and had deep-set blue eyes, a white beard, and bushy white brows. He looked like Moses. He should have been holding a stone tablet in his hands. He seemed years older than his wife. She had the appearance of a gray mouse and wore clothing to match.

The girl, Phemy, was pale and quiet. She sat with folded hands, scarce moving. When she did raise her eyes, I saw something in them I could not name. It put me on notice.

I turned the corn cakes on the griddle. Daddy and Mama had gone upstairs for a minute, likely to say a proper hello.

I poured coffee for the reverend and his wife. They thanked me. I looked at Phemy. "Would you like tea? Or milk?"

She did not answer.

"She's weary," the mouse wife said. "The trip over the mountains." She said no more, but I knew.

All that bouncing in the wagon, the narrow trails, the places where there are no roads, the wild beasts that cry in the night, the sight of bears and rattlesnakes, the woods that close in on you, the wolves and wildcats that scream at night, the mountains that go on forever with no other humans in sight.

And I could name what I saw in Phemy's eyes. Fear. Strong women have gone mad on such trips and have had to be taken back once they got here.

"I'll make tea." I got out the white pot and poured hot water into it. I set out tea and fetched a piece of my custard pastry. I know you shouldn't eat it for breakfast. But Phemy looked like she needed, bad, to do something she wasn't supposed to do.

She didn't thank me. I turned back to the corn cakes.

"Why are you crying?" I heard Ann ask.

I turned from the hearth. Large tears were coming down Phemy's face. Ann was standing next to her, staring.

"Nothing dries sooner than a tear," Ann said.

I grabbed her and pulled her next to me. I smiled at the mouse wife. "Ann repeats things. It's a quote from Benjamin Franklin. Mama is fond of him."

"I never *wanted* to come!" Phemy whispered savagely to her sister. "You would have it, though, wouldn't you?"

"We want what's best for you," the reverend told her.

"My folks are dead," the mouse wife explained to me. "I could have left my sister with my aunt in Kentucky. But we thought she'd be better with us."

"I didn't *want* to come," Phemy said again.

"Hush and mind your manners," the reverend boomed. Phemy hushed.

Even James wouldn't scold me like that in front of strangers, I thought. Oh, he'd give me the rough side of his tongue if I sassed Mama, yes. But he'd take me outside and do it in private. And Phemy can't sass the reverend like I do James. How can you sass Moses?

It gave me no pause that the woman was so mousy. Likely he boomed at her that way, too.

I piled corn cakes on the plate. I thought Phemy a rude little piece. Is that what comes from having no brothers? Still, I felt sorry for her.

121

"Rebecca." The door opened and Will stood there. "Come see what James brought you."

"Me?"

"A present," Will said. And the door banged behind him.

Mama and Daddy came down the stairs. Daddy smiled, took the plate of corn cakes from me, set it on the table, and kissed me. "Wasn't it your birthday a fortnight ago?"

I nodded.

He smelled of woodsmoke, tobacco, horses, and leather. "Well, if you haven't grown another inch. Mama told me how you persuaded Mrs. Maxwell to go to the speech. I'm right proud of you, Rebecca. You're Mama's mainstay. Go on now, see what your brother has for you."

I went outside. My brothers were standing around the wagon. Will was holding a small sack, and James took it from him. "This is for you, Rebecca," he said.

The sack was soft and open on top. I peered in.

A fluffy gray kitten with green eyes and white under its chin was looking up at me. I felt a rush of disbelief. Then tenderness. I looked up. All my brothers were grinning. I couldn't speak. I lifted the kitten out of the sack and held it close. Tears came to my eyes. It was purring.

"I've brought another for Martha," James said. "Yours is a male, hers a female. When they get older

122

you can breed them. It's what you said we needed to be civilized out here, isn't it?"

I looked at James. Well, I thought, of all people! James.

"Thank you," I said.

He nodded. "How's Harmony?"

"I haven't ridden her yet today. She needs a good run."

"She's ridden her every day, though," Will told him. "And taken right good care of her."

"Good. I'll saddle her now and ride over to Martha's. Tell Mama I'll be home for supper." He took another bundle from the wagon. From in the sack I heard a meow.

I stood holding the kitten, soft against me. I'd forgotten how soft cats can be. How needful of you. Yet how they can be strong and defend themselves when they must. I'd forgotten a lot of things I used to know.

My brothers went inside. I stood pondering. Is that what Phemy was afraid of? That she was soft from life in Kentucky? And wouldn't be able to protect herself out here if the need arose?

James came out of the barn on Harmony, and I ran over to him. "She looks like you took care of her right fine," he said.

"James?" I looked up at him.

"Yes?"

"The girl, Phemy. She's not happy."

123

"I know."

"She's right scared. She doesn't like it here."

"She lost her horse on the way here. He was her favorite. It took sick and we did everything we could to save it, but we couldn't. Why don't you talk to her?"

"What could I say?"

"That it takes some getting used to, living out here. But she can do it."

I nodded. "Thank you."

"You already said that."

Not for the kitten, I wanted to say. For not being like old Moses. But I didn't say it. He nodded, pressed his heels into Harmony's side, and rode off. Well, of all the people, I thought. James.

"Does she have to sleep there?" Sitting on my bed, Phemy looked down disdainfully at Ann, who was asleep, bundled in the trundle bed on the side of mine.

"She sleeps next to me every night."

"At home I have a room of my own."

"I'll have one someday," I said.

She looked around the small room Ann and I shared. I have to admit that by the sputtering candlelight it didn't look very commodious. "This is a log house," she said.

"My daddy and George built it when we first came. George was only sixteen. It's well daubed with clay. It's warm in winter. We have wood and food in great

124

plenty. My daddy and brothers make much of the ground and the woods."

"At home I lived in a good frame house."

"We don't calculate to live in this house forever. Daddy and my brothers are going to build a new one soon."

She nodded. "Why did you come here?"

"Slavery back in Kentucky," I said. "My people are against it. We don't have slavery here."

"You don't have slavery, but you have a law that is a foul blot on your books."

"What law?"

"That blacks or mulattoes can't testify in court against whites. Ever."

"It isn't true," I said.

"Isn't it? Why don't you ask your brother James. He seems to know everything."

I hated her at that moment. Something was grinding at her innards, and she was lashing out at everything because of it. Likely it was her horse. Why didn't she speak of him?

"I'm not going to stay here," she said. "I hate it. Everything about it. You have no school, do you?"

"We're getting one soon."

"Yes, for five- and ten-year-olds. Show me your best dress. What you wear of a Sunday when you go to meeting."

"We don't go to meeting. We have no minister.

125

Which is why my daddy made the trip to get your brother-in-law."

"At home we go to church. There are horses hitched all along the fence, and men and women come from all around. Everyone shakes hands, and people stroll and talk, and we eat afterward under the trees. You don't have a church. Where do you expect my brother-in-law to preach?"

I had no answer for her.

"Show me your best dress anyway," she pushed.

I went to the small trunk under the window, opened it, and pulled out my calico.

"Just as I thought. Mine is a green silk." She jumped off the bed and went to her own trunk.

Never had I seen such a dress! It had flounces and was trimmed with black ribbon! My mouth watered. Tears came to my eyes.

"You see?" She held up the dress. Her eyes glittered maliciously. "And I've got a bonnet to match it, too."

Talk to her, James had said.

"I'd admire for you to stay, Phemy. We can be friends. We have a lot of books. And Mama plays the violin. Mrs. Maxwell, my friend, has a pianoforte, and she's quality. She teaches me all kinds of things."

"I'm not staying," she said. She lay down under the quilt and stared at the ceiling.

"How will you go back?"

"Heard your daddy and brother talking about a family named Turner. Said they were planning a trip back this fall. Before the snows come. I'll ask to go with them."

"Will your people let you go?"

"They'll have to. My brother-in-law will be busy with his preaching. That means my sister will have to do all the work herself. I heard your daddy say good help is hard to come by out here. I'm not hoeing my brother-in-law's corn or making his soap or milking his cows. I'll die first."

"Tell me about your horse," I said.

She sat upright. "How did you know?"

"My brother told me he died."

"It isn't that he *died*. It's *how*. He was taken sick. When we camped for the night, they tried to save him but couldn't. He groaned all night. But it wasn't even *that*."

"What was it, then?"

"The wolves."

"The wolves?"

"Yes. They knew he was dying. They waited in the woods, howling all night like demons. The only thing that kept them from rushing us was the fires. Never have I spent such a night. In the morning my horse died. And we had to leave him."

"Oh," I said.

127

"I hate this wilderness. I hate everything about it."

"We're happy here," I said. "People can be happy here."

"Are you?"

"Yes."

"Look how worn down your mama looks."

"She isn't worn down."

"You don't think so? Then you don't know the difference anymore."

"My mama's happy," I said vehemently. "She has pride. But it isn't an offense to others. She keeps her own counsel, but that doesn't mean she doesn't know what she's about. She knows her mind. And speaks it, and we all reverence her."

"She's still worn down."

"At least she's not mousy like your sister!" I blurted the words out. Then I snuffed the candle and snuggled under my own covering on the floor.

In the dark, in a little while, I heard three sounds. Ann's breathing, a wolf howling outside in the distance, and Phemy's quiet sobs.

I was sorry I'd yelled at her. But what could I do? She'd attacked Mama. I couldn't allow that.

Then her voice came across the darkness. "You hear that? Wolves!"

"All I hear is Ann's breathing. It's a comfort to me. I'm used to wolves howling at night."

"You're savage. Everybody out here is."

"Maybe," I said.

"Well, I'm going back. Before my sister gets worn down and I don't know the difference anymore. And before I get used to the wolves."

The Armstrongs stayed with us two days, then went to board with the Maxwells. A week later Phemy left with the Turners, who were to spend the winter in Kentucky.

"I'm sore afflicted that I couldn't make a friend of Phemy," I told Mama.

"The things which hurt, instruct," she said.

Benjamin Franklin again. "Now what does that mean?"

"Learn from this and the pain will lessen. We can't make everyone love us. Trying will pure wear us out. It's the hardest thing you'll ever have to learn."

"Did you learn it when you were my age, Mama?"

But she gave the conversation a new turn. "Your daddy's going to tell it at supper tonight. He's been named the first county treasurer. And James, the first county surveyor. Your daddy will be in charge of collecting taxes. James will be surveying to lay out the roads."

She was cleaning a catfish Sam had caught. I was making the stuffing. It would feed us all tonight. I looked at her. She didn't seem worn down to me. She seemed right perky since Daddy was back, matter of fact. Was it possible I didn't know the difference anymore?

"I think Phemy couldn't help the way she was, Mama. Losing her horse on the way here set her against us and our ways."

"Some people have lost children on the way west and stayed," she answered simply.

I looked at her again. She *accepted* things. And just went on. I wasn't like Phemy, no. But I could never be like Mama, either. Could I?

"I want to name my kitten Moses," I told her.

"And why such a name?"

"With the white under his chin, he reminds me of Reverend Armstrong. And he looks like Moses to me."

"I suppose it's all right. As long as you reverence Mr. Armstrong," she said.

CHAPTER 11

August–November 1804

"*Hold still, Ann, I want to brush* your hair and put a ribbon in it."

"I don't want to be sprinkled, Rebecca."

"You have to."

"Why?"

All Ann asked these days was why. She was five. Well, you couldn't tell a five-year-old that being sprinkled will keep her from the grip of Satan. Though betimes I was convinced Ann had the devil in her. "Because it will make Mama happy," I said. "And because finally your name will truly be yours."

"Whose was it before?"

"Hold still," I said. "Besides, you have to give good

example to Andrew, even though he's older. He's to be sprinkled, too."

"And the baby?"

"Yes."

"But he's only three weeks old. He's too small."

"No. It's right for him to be sprinkled now. You and Andrew had to wait too long."

"I don't like Reverend Armstrong. He bellows."

"Hush. He's a reverend. He has a right to bellow."

"He told Daddy that George and Sam are headed for perdition because they're building the still for Daddy to make whiskey. Where's perdition?"

"It's a place reverends want to send people who don't do what they like. He doesn't hold with drinking whiskey."

"Is it like hell?"

"It's on the way there."

"Like the Bullskin Trace is on the way to Detroit?"

"Yes."

"I heard Reverend tell Daddy that we should use our Indian corn for bread and puddings and cakes. Daddy told him whiskey isn't as important as bread, but this is a new country. And chills and fever take us sometimes. And we need the whiskey for medicine."

"That's right. Daddy's right."

"It didn't matter. The reverend said Daddy is supplying temptation. Then Daddy told him nobody around here drinks too much, but they do pass the jug around at logrollings and house-raisings."

"Daddy's right about that, too."

"The reverend said Daddy should keep the whiskey under lock and key when people come to build Will's house."

"When did you hear all this?" What a little busybody she was. She chattered like a parrot, and you couldn't say a thing in front of her but that she repeated it.

"Last Sunday after meeting. I was with Daddy when they were talking. Reverend doesn't like it that James raced Harmony in Cincinnati last fall, either. And won all that money. He says Daddy shouldn't let James race this fall."

"Well, there isn't much Reverend can do about it. Too many people like their racing. And James does pretty much what he likes."

"James's Martha is coming today. She says I'll be the prettiest girl in her daddy's school."

"Likely you will be."

"You aren't going to school in the fall?"

"No."

"I heard James tell Mama you should."

"Well, we've yet to settle it, James and I. Thing he has to realize is that I do pretty much what I like, too. Now you just stand still while I put a ribbon in your hair. You have to look nice. Don't forget, this is the first baptism in Greene County."

"And it's in our barn."

"Yes, people are coming from all over, so you must look nice. They're going to be paying special mind to you and Andrew and little Anthony."

"Is Mama going to have more babies?"

"Now why should you ask such a thing?"

"I don't want her to. I want to be the littlest girl."

"I always wanted that, too. Then you came along."

"Are you sorry?"

"No. But I don't think you need worry. Mama told me she's past the time now for more babies. Anthony is her last."

There was nothing for it. I had to go with James to Mr. Townsley's house. It was the only way to settle this school thing between us.

We'd been fussing at one another too long now about it. We had a fight the night of the little ones' sprinkling, after all the company left. And the next morning we started again at breakfast.

"Make this thing right between you," Daddy said. "I don't care how. Rebecca, if you have the mettle to stand up to James, then you've got the mettle to prove to him, somehow, that you don't need Mr. Townsley's school."

"How?" I asked.

"I don't care how. It's bringing dissension to our family. I won't have it."

"Why don't we let Mr. Townsley decide?" Mama asked.

"Good idea," James said. "We'll ride over today. Let him fire some questions at you. He's the teacher. What say you, Rebecca?"

"Today?" My face went white. "What questions?"

"Whatever he chooses," James said. "I'll stay out of it. And I'll abide by his decision. If he thinks you don't need schooling, I won't badger you anymore. Fair enough?"

Blood pounded in my ears. Here was a way to have an end of it. But could I do it? "Daddy?" I asked.

"Whatever you want, Rebecca. But if Mr. Townsley says you do need schooling, you go. No fussing."

"Isn't it a bit unfair to Rebecca and Mr. Townsley?" Mama asked. "Neither one of them is prepared."

"It's better that way," Daddy said. "The best battles are won under surprise attacks."

"Mama? What'll I do?" I appealed.

"Go put on your good blue calico and remember everything I taught you," she said.

I went. Problem was, Daddy didn't say which side had won those best battles.

"Well, young lady, so I'm to see how much you know," Mr. Townsley said.

Martha brought a tray of tea and set it down on a table in the best room. James took a chair. His hat was in his hands. Was he going to stay? He was. He was fixing to settle in. At least Martha had the sense to leave.

"Pour yourself a cup of tea there," Mr. Townsley said. "You know arithmetic?"

"My mama taught me."

He sat down at his desk in the corner. "Well, I'll just make up a little paper here for you to work on while you sip your tea. James? Why don't you join Martha in the garden? It's a nice day."

James went. Thank heaven he listened to his soon-to-be father-in-law.

Mr. Townsley scratch-scratch-scratched at that paper with his pen. It sounded just like a chicken in our farmyard, and I began to wish, more and more, that I was there right now, collecting the eggs for Mama. Oh, why had I agreed to do this?

He signaled I should come to the desk. "See if you can do these sums. They're from *Dilworth's Arithmetic*." He pulled out the chair for me.

I sat and stared at the paper. Addition. Ciphering. Multiplication. I set myself to the task, pretending I was home at our kitchen table and Mama was readying supper.

Mr. Townsley paced. The clock ticked. I worked all

the sums. When I was finished, he took the paper and made sounds like he had quinsy throat. "Where did you learn all this?"

"My mama taught me."

More sounds.

"Hot tea with a little honey in it helps the throat," I said.

"Is that a fact?"

"Yessir. I learned that from my mama, too."

"This mama of yours taught you quite a bit, then, did she? What do you know of history?"

"I've read Clarendon's *History of England*. I've read *Rollins Ancient History*."

He nodded. "Can you explain to me the principles of the Declaration of Independence?"

I thought for a moment. "Yessir."

"Do so."

"I don't recollect all the proper wording."

"Never mind the proper wording. Tell me what you think it means."

"Well, sir, we were fussing at each other, us and England. The way James and I are doing now. And we wanted to go it on our own and prove to them that we're as good as them, and if they gave us a chance, maybe better. Besides which, we wanted to teach them that nobody, not even if he is king, can take away our rights. And we weren't going to hold with kings anymore. We wanted to come and go as we please and do things our way. Only they wouldn't hear of it, and they kept badgering us."

"How?"

"Well, they did all those acts. Sugar and quartering and stamps."

"Explain the Quartering Act to me."

"Well, sir, they wanted to be able to put their soldiers in our houses. Without so much as a by-your-leave. Just move them right in. Can you picture it? Our house is crowded enough now. Could you just see us with a British officer sleeping in the book room? Even Benjamin Franklin said that fish and visitors stink after three days."

"What was the Stamp Act?"

"A pretty mess. They wanted every piece of paper we used to carry the seal of the Crown. And, of course, we had to pay for the privilege! And then there was the business with the tea. Again they wanted to tax us. For tea! Onerous! It was just to badger us. Just like James is doing to me about school. And so we said let's get together and tell them to leave us be. And so we got Mr. Jefferson, who's president now, to write us a declaration. Then we had to follow through on it, and so we fought the war. And lots of good men like my daddy left their homes to do it. And many died."

I stopped talking. I felt silly. Why was he looking at

me like that? He seemed kind of pale, like he was getting the ague.

"It has all kinds of fancy language in it, but that's about the gist of it," I told him. "'Course, Mr. Jefferson, being from Virginia, is a high-toned man."

"Yes, indeed. Ah, would you care to tell me what else your mama has taught you?"

"John Locke," I said. "He said, 'We know heat because we have felt fire. We know white because we have seen sugar or snow.' I always thought that was tricky of him to compare sugar and snow. They do look alike, don't they? Especially of a winter morning when the snow's just fallen all clean in our farmyard."

"Yes. Of course. Who else can you quote?"

"Isaac Watts, who wrote about logic. 'Do not let your soul be a looking glass, that wheresoever you turn it receives the images of all objects but retains none.' And Burgersdyk, the Dutch theorist, said, 'Let Democritus feign that truth lies hidden at the bottom of a well. Logic will dive and fetch it out.' Sort of reminds me how our dog, Shag, dives right into the river sometimes and fetches out a fish. I see that fish in his mouth and I just think about truth. Do you think it's wrong to compare the truth to a fish, Mr. Townsley?"

"Not at all. No. Do you know who Isaac Newton was?"

"Yessir. He defined gravity. And Tycho Brahe was

the great Danish astronomer who first said the sun revolved around the earth. Astronomy has to do with the stars and all the heavenly bodies. And do you know what Tecumtha told me? He said the Shawnees call the northern lights the dancing ghosts."

"Tecumseh?"

"Yessir. He visits us. I'm teaching him to read. Oh, he *does* read, after a fashion. But he wants to learn more."

"You're teaching him."

"Yessir."

"What else have you to tell me, Rebecca?"

"Well, let's see. I've read Gravesande's *Natural Philosophy*. He was a Dutchman and a pupil of Newton's. His work is in two folio volumes. My daddy has them in his book room. They've got drawings and engravings of pendulums and siphons. He writes about air and what he calls other elastic fluids. He writes about the construction of the eye. Eyes are strange things, Mr. Townsley. My brothers go on fire hunts and shine the eyes of deer at night. I went along once. There is no more beautiful sight than when a deer shines its eyes."

He was silent for a long moment. Just stood there looking out the window to where James had joined Martha in the kitchen garden. "Tell me about the French War. Do you know what happened on the Plains of Abraham?"

"Yessir. A great battle was fought. It happened in July of 1759. The French were holding onto Quebec tighter than my cat, Moses, holds onto a mouse he's caught in the barn. And the English had to take it."

"Why?"

"Well, because for nigh onto seventy-five years the French had sent Indians down from there to raid us. And it was destroying our farms and getting our people killed. So Mr. Pitt of England sent us James Wolfe. And we sent twenty thousand men up the St. Lawrence quicker than you could say, 'God save George the Second.' The French had General Montcalm, and they fought Wolfe on the Plains of Abraham. But the English and Americans won, and so we were freed of the yoke of the French. 'Course after that it gets a bit confusing."

"Oh? Why's that?"

"Because in the last war it was the French that helped us whip the English. Mama says think of it as a chess game. Clear off the board after the French war and put different figures back on for the next. She says men never get tired of playing chess."

"Yes, that's right. Now can you tell me what's happened this year that everyone is talking about?"

I studied on the question a moment. "That depends, Mr. Townsley. My brothers are talking about how Aaron Burr shot Alexander Hamilton in a duel in New Jersey. George says that if Hamilton had a good Kentucky rifle, Burr never would have bested him. But it's all they talk about. Of course, I heard some people at Gowdy's Mercantile last week arguing over whether Lewis and Clark really could find a waterway to take them all the way to the Pacific Ocean. It's up for conjecture, you know."

"Yes." He sat down. He took out a handkerchief and wiped his brow. "Anything else?"

"Well, sir, just one more thing. Mrs. Maxwell has taught me a lot, too. She told me why Sir William Howe never quite caught up with General Washington when he was retreating across the Jerseys. Do you want to know why?"

"Do tell."

"Well, you see, Howe had a mistress. After Mrs. Maxwell told me about her, I studied up on it. Her name was Betsey Loring. She had a husband, but Howe made him Commissioner of Prisons to keep him busy. Well, it seems Howe couldn't bear to leave Mrs. Loring long enough to pursue Washington on time. He was always late. And so Washington kept getting away. Aren't we lucky that Howe had Mrs. Loring?"

He stood up. He had a funny look on his face. I did think he was coming down with an ague. He was looking a mite pale. He went outside to get James, and after a while both of them came through the door and looked at me.

"You don't have to go to school, Rebecca," James said. And he had the same look on his face.

My, I thought, I hope that ague isn't catching.

Near three months later Will married Elizabeth Pomeroy. Daddy said the harvest had to be in first. House-raisings and weddings take all a body's time and strength.

Will's was the first wedding in our new log church. He was the first of Mama's children to wed. And Elizabeth was the first bound person to be freed of her indenture since we'd become a state.

Three firsts. When the women were preparing the wedding feast, Reverend Armstrong's mousy wife said we should look for a fourth. Three is bad luck. Only *she* would say that. But it set me to thinking.

Not that we're a superstitious lot. But everybody knows that if a dog crosses a hunter's path he'll come home empty-handed, that a dog baying at an old moon means death, and that the sight of a sloughed-off snakeskin means strong, evil forces are about.

For the last month neighbors had been helping build Will's house. Some mixed the mortar for daubing the cracks, some hauled the stones for the chimney. Some were choppers, to fell the trees, others cut them at proper lengths. Owen Davis used his team of oxen to haul the cut logs. But for some reason he couldn't manage them well enough.

My brother George said it was because he didn't swear at them. George was right. He took them in hand and sweared properlike and the oxen hauled just fine.

But swearing is a violation of the law. And so Sheriff Maxwell had to fine him fifty cents each time he did it.

By the time all the logs were hauled for Will's house, George owed five dollars. The housewarming itself pure wore everybody out. People danced all night.

The wedding day dawned bright and blue, one of the last true warm days of November. Mama filled my brothers with hominy, eggs, ham, and coffee. Twice I saw her pat Will's shoulder as she passed by him.

It came time to set off to get Will to church. George picked up John, and James grabbed Andrew.

"Leave them. They can go on with us," Mama said.

"This is men's business, Mama," James said. "They have to learn. I'd take Anthony if you'd let me."

John was ten, Andrew eight. James set Andrew in front of him on Harmony. I let John ride Saxony.

Everything went just fine with the wedding. Elizabeth wore a new calico and shawl. Never have I seen two people as happy. They stared into each other's eyes as if they could drink each other's souls.

Everybody marched from the log church down on Massie's Creek to Will and Elizabeth's new house on the piece of land Daddy gave them near the creek that crosses Yellow Springs Pike.

The men led their horses in double file. The women had put fall flowers on the bridles. Halfway there, the men stopped and fired their muskets to cover the bride and groom with smoke so they could sneak a kiss. The horses all sprang about then, of course, and the women shrieked.

The women had worked for days on the bridal feast. Beef, pork, fowl, venison, potatoes, cabbage, vegetables, Indian corn, all kinds of pies, puddings, custard pastry. Barrels of cider and whiskey. Mama's best pewter was laid out on a trestle table under the trees. And when we found there were more people than pewter spoons, someone brought out some old-type spoons made of horns.

After we ate, the dancing commenced. We did four-handed reels, square sets, and jigs. Sometimes a man and woman would jig off to dance alone. Or do some spooning. Discovered missing, they were hunted up, paraded back onto the dance floor, and then the fiddler played "Hang On Till Tomorrow Morning." Then they had to dance alone.

The dance floor was Mama's carpet. We brought it from home and laid it out under the trees.

Once I danced with Will. "I've never seen you so happy," I told him.

"I've waited all these years, Rebecca," he said. "Waited to grow up. Waited for Elizabeth to grow up. Waited to have her indenture finished, then for Pa to say I could wed, then for our house to be built. It's why I'm happy. No more waiting."

Around nine o'clock was time to steal the bride. Martha Townsley came over and got me to help. I felt proud. Because the older girls in the community considered me grown now.

Our job was to get Elizabeth into the house, up the ladder to the loft, out of her dress, into her nightshift, and into their bed. Well, a lot of giggling went on. And the older women said some things in front of me that made me blush to hear. But Elizabeth didn't mind. She seemed to like all the fuss.

No one will ever do such to me when I marry, I vowed. But then it was an empty vow. For I should never marry.

After we did that, the men got Will into the house and up the ladder. Then the dancing went on. The little ones went to sleep right on the ground, wrapped in blankets. All except Ann. She wouldn't settle in. She ran around all night, flitting between the dancers like a June bug.

As the night went on, James reminded the rest of

my brothers that the bride and groom must stand in need of some refreshments. "I've got black betty," he said. So into the house they went again to prop up the ladder and send up black betty, which was a bottle of liquor.

Then around midnight, George came over to James, who was talking to Mr. Townsley. "I heard the mules braying," he said.

James rounded up Sam and some others and disappeared into the darkness outside the circle of torchlight. In a little bit we heard yelping, like Indian war whoops. And gunshots.

Aaron Beall hadn't been invited. Nor had Ben Kizer. Nobody wanted fights at the wedding. But it's the custom; those not invited take offense and, for revenge, cut off the manes, foretops, and tails of the horses of those in the wedding company.

Beall and Kizer, who'd near killed each other that day at the courthouse, had now joined forces. But James had been expecting this. So where the horses should have been he'd put the team of oxen Owen Davis had given Will to help him clear his fields.

Can oxen work with shorn-off tails?

When we got home Ann was still fired up. She went chasing off after Shag. I ran through the wet grass to find her.

She was under some trees behind the house. "Look

what I found, Rebecca." She held up a piece of sloughed-off snakeskin. "I found it this morning and hid it here. Can I take it inside with me?"

"Put that down," I scolded. And I slapped her hand, sharp. She cried, and I carried her into the house.

When Mama asked what happened I said, "Nothing. She's tired and unruly."

Sometimes I think I'm getting like James.

CHAPTER 12

Autumn 1805

❦

Nobody thought anything of it when Reverend Armstrong came to ask my father or brothers whether apples or peach trees were best to plant on his improvement, what to do when his cow had colic, or when to sow his turnip and pea seeds.

The reverend could quote Revelation word for word, but he didn't know you could reap your first harvest of cucumbers by June fifteenth. If my father and brothers did not educate him in the ways of farming, he and his mouse wife would have starved while he went about preaching about eating manna in the wilderness.

So when he came in early October to ask George to make him a pair of stilts, nobody thought anything of it. Until he told us what they were for.

"I need them to cross Massie's Creek in times of high water," he said. "I always walk the four miles to church. But that river is in my way. If I had stilts, I could cross it and not get wet."

Daddy said his worldly circumstances did not yet allow him to have a horse. Mama said let's loan him one. Daddy said no, his pride won't allow him to have a horse, either. His pride just about allows him to accept a side of venison from us on occasion. Or some hocks of Indian corn for his cow.

George thought him pure daft, but made him the stilts anyway. George will make anything out of wood for anybody. He built a contraption for Sam to get sap out of our sugar maples, didn't he? One barrel of sap makes five pounds of sugar. Sam and I made fifty pounds of sugar last spring. Still, when I came upon George carving the stilts I heard him mumbling. "Why doesn't he just ask God to part the waters?" I thought it was blasphemous. I also thought it was funny.

My heart was heavy riding home from Elizabeth and Will's house, though the sky was the color of a delft plate, the trees were like something burning on the hills, and in two weeks I would be fourteen.

On the surface, life was good. Squirrels didn't get the corn before husking, we had no green caterpillars to strip the land that year, we got thirty bushels of barley to the acre, and the rains quenched the thirst of the wheat field without drowning it before harvest. Baby Anthony was fat and saucy, James was away most of the time surveying, John, Andrew, and Ann were in school and didn't plague me during the day. George and Sam were busy with the fall harvest. Mama let me proceed with my studies at my own will, and I was reading *Paradise Lost*.

But life was not lived on the surface. If it were, the world would have been as it appeared before my eyes that moment, all golden and lush and perfect. The reverend would have had a horse, Phemy would have stayed and I would have had a friend, people wouldn't have been walking around saying that Lewis and Clark were lost to us forever, and Will's Elizabeth would not have been dying.

I had just been to visit. Will told us she was down with the stomach complaint that plagued so many that year. George said even the Indians had it up north. Said he heard some Shawnees died of it.

I went that day and found Elizabeth huddled under her quilt, with dark moons under her eyes and skin like parchment. Will was working his fields, and the house was in disarray. She had not even been able to get herself a cup of broth.

I made some broth and left it in the pot on the hearth. I neatened the house. I made her tea with honey.

"She'll be fine," Will told me when I walked across the field to speak to him. "She's a stout body."

She wasn't. Will was being blind. He had cornhusks on his eyes. Elizabeth was dying. I thought she knew it. And I thought Will knew it, too.

I could not go home just yet. For I'd have to tell Mama about Elizabeth. I would put it off for a while. Words spoken make something true. I would tarry a bit, down by the creek.

Saxony knew the way. I was just about to slip from her back and pick some purple wildflowers to bring home to Mama when I saw movement in Massie's Creek.

What was I seeing? And then I knew. Reverend Armstrong on his stilts.

I stood watching, holding Saxony's reins. The creek ran clear and inviting. Both Saxony and I wanted a drink. But I would wait to see how the good reverend did on his stilts.

He was perched on them. In his black reverend clothing, he looked like a scarecrow. His coattails flapped in the wind. The waters of Massie's Creek were middling high, for we'd had our share of autumn rains.

He looked like baby Anthony trying to walk. He wobbled, he weaved. Only he had nothing to grab onto. A rush of wind blew off his hat and his white hair stood on end and made him look like a demented

Moses as he tried to sidestep the rocks. I held my breath. Carefully he raised up first one stilt then the other. His progress was slow and painful.

He looked so out of place there in the middle of the creek. The stark blackness of him made him stand out like an alien thing. Like he did not belong here. Then, of a sudden, a piece of tree branch came floating at him, knocked into the stilts, and set him off balance.

He cried out. "Thou dids't divide the sea through Thy power; Thou breakest the heads of the dragons in the waters!"

You would think there were dragons in the waters for all the difficulty he was having. A flock of birds took flight from a nearby tree when he yelled. They swirled in confusion overhead. Then, just as he was about to fall, he righted himself.

On the other side of Massie's Creek I saw something. A figure on horseback. Someone else was privy to this scene, too, hidden in the trees, watching. Who?

As I was pondering it, the reverend went on, step by step, until he got to the other side, where he jumped off his stilts, gathered them in, tucked them under one arm, and went on his way. As if walking across a creek in the middle of the day on stilts in the middle of Ohio was nothing.

He never looked up. He never saw the figure on horseback half concealed behind the trees. Part of them and the landscape. Even part of the creek and the sky. Like he belonged there. He never saw the red-tailed hawk screeching overhead. I did.

I waved, climbed on Saxony, and rode out into the middle of the creek. He met me there.

"You're back," I said.

"Hello, Gal-o-weh girl." He smiled at me. He seemed browner than ever, leaner than ever, sadder than ever. I stared at him. The feather he wore in the red band on his head stood out, etched against the blue sky. His hair shone. The thrust of his jaw, the depth of his eyes, the squareness of his shoulders, his smile, everything cut into some place inside me I had not known could be cut into until now.

I'm bleeding, I thought. Inside me I'm cut and bleeding because he has come back and the joy of it is so sharp. And I know he'll go away again. And already I feel the pain.

"Where have you *been?*"

We sat our horses in the middle of Massie's Creek. Water swirled around us. They drank. The warm October sun felt good on my shoulders.

"To the northeast. To Pennsylvania. To Canada. Back to Chicago. To the lands beyond the shining mountains, to Minnesota country."

"Why?"

"To speak to all the Indians. Even to the Omahas and the Iowas on the other side of the mother of all waters."

I nodded. The Mississippi. "Like Lewis and Clark."

He nodded. "The long-knife captains."

"They're lost," I said. "No one has heard from them. President Jefferson's experiment is a failure."

"No. I have spoken to those who have met them."

I felt a thrill of joy. "They're *alive?*"

"They are building their council fires everywhere. Telling the Sioux they will soon be living under their Jefferson father."

"I'm so glad! Everyone else will be, too." I wondered if Josh had caught up with Lewis and Clark.

He scowled. "O-hio is now the seventeenth fire," he said.

"Yes. We became a state."

"Soon Indiana country will be a fire. They have a governor man now. Like O-hio had before it became a state. Harrison. He had his people get five chiefs of the Sacs drunk. Then they sign a treaty and hand over much of our land."

I nodded. My daddy had told me. Fifty-one million acres in the Mississippi valley.

"This is why I travel. The Mohawks, Oneidas, Winnebagos, Wyandots, Ottawas, Sacs, Kickapoos, Senecas, *all* tribes must set down their quarrels and work together. In a union. Like the seventeen fires. Or the great tide of Shemanese who follow the long-knife captains will push them into the sea."

"And you want to stop them."

"We must. Or we will be no more."

His eyes met mine. And I understood his sadness. His people and mine could never be friends. He knew it and had made himself the anointed leader to tell them such.

Now I knew it. Had he come to tell me? No. He'd come as a friend.

He grinned. "Why was that man walking on long wooden legs?"

"He's our new reverend. He doesn't have a horse. It's his way of crossing the creek at high water."

"He is a holy man?"

"Yes."

"Then why doesn't he ask your God to part the waters?"

I laughed. It was so good to have him back! "That's what George says."

We turned our horses in the direction of home.

"George made the stilts," I told him. "I wanted him to make me a canoe so I can paddle down the river. For my birthday last week, he made me a dower chest."

"What is this dower chest?"

"To put linens in. For when I wed. Only I'm never going to wed. But it's lovely anyway. I put my fancys in it."

"What is this fancys?"

"My journal that I'm writing in. The silver bracelet you gave me. A drawing Ann made for me at school. A cornhusk doll from when I was small. George just got back from a trip to Dayton where he helped build a house for Colonel Patterson. The harvest is in. Daddy is the tax collector, we have a new baby, and Will married his Elizabeth near a year ago. But she's sick. And I think she's dying. She has the stomach sickness."

He told me of his life. "I have been to the village of Tawa on the Auglaize River. Change of Feathers has died of the white man's stomach sickness. He was a great prophet. I told my brother, Loud Noise, to tell the people that three would die and the other come well."

"You had a vision," I said.

"Yes. Until now Loud Noise has not been able to make the different tribes believe in my plan to come together. He has been taken with drink and greed. But he, too, got a bad sickness when he went away to a far place and had a vision. When he returned from this place, he made a great speech at Tawa. Words came from his mouth like fire and burned into my people. He no more takes the white man's whiskey. He keeps himself clean. He calls himself Open Door now and has taken on duties of prophet."

"But you told him what to say."

He nodded solemnly. "But he now has powers as big as mine. And he believes himself. This is much important. And makes others believe in him. And in me."

"Did the people recover at Tawa, as you said?"

"Yes."

We rode slowly through our cornfield, past the cattle feasting on the stalks. "You can predict things," I said.

"Yes."

"George told me that three years ago you predicted a great earthquake will come."

"Yes."

"When?"

"That is not important. It will be a sign. When it comes, my people will know there will no longer be many different tribes. Only Indians."

I reined in Saxony. "Mr. Tecumtha, there is something I need to know before we get to the house. Before my brothers take you away from me."

"Yes, Gal-o-weh girl."

"George says you're as good as the almanac. Or as my daddy who knows when it will rain because of the bullet in his neck."

He smiled.

"Can you tell me if Will's Elizabeth is going to die?"

He looked solemn. "We speak of this, Gal-o-weh girl. But not now," he said.

"When?"

"Much time. We will speak of it." Then he grinned again. "I have learned the these-those words. You will see."

"Yes. You speak very well, Mr. Tecumtha."

"I have read the Bible your father gave me. Now you tell me something. This war in heaven, when Chief Michael fought the dragons. It was great war, was it not?"

"Yes. Michael and his angels fought Satan. And cast him out of heaven forever."

"I will tell my people about this Chief Michael," he said.

He stayed for three weeks.

Again the wigewa went up in the wheat field, though it was October and the nights brought frost. Mornings, when I did my chores, he went off to the nearby woods. To hunt. Or fish. Or to have visions.

Along about two in the afternoon, when I'd spent two hours at my books and Mama had taken up some mending and before the little ones were home from school, he came to the door.

Always he brought some offering. Rock bass or sunfish he'd caught. Sweet potatoes wrapped in corn husks that he would set in our hearth to bake over the fire. A small bow and arrow he'd made for John.

One afternoon he brought cold water root for Elizabeth.

She now had a fever. Mama and I walked across the fields to visit her every evening. Owen Davis had sent his sister to stay. She knew midwifery and had attended Mama when Ann and Anthony were born. But all her decoctions had not worked and Elizabeth was still failing.

Tecumseh showed Mama how to prepare the cold water root. "The fever will be gone in five days," he told her.

Every day when he came, he asked after Elizabeth. Mama told him the fever was gone but she was growing weaker. He grew solemn. Had he expected Elizabeth to come well again like the Shawnees at Tawa?

Had he made a prophecy that had not worked?

I did not ask. When he came we read Shakespeare. We read the *Life of George Washington* by John Marshall. He was much taken with Washington. "Many prisoners he took at Tren-ton," he told me.

"Nine hundred." I said. "My daddy was in Lancaster when they were marched through. He counted them."

He liked best the story of Washington freezing at Valley Forge. And holding out against the British.

I told him how Thomas Jefferson was elected president again last December, how Daddy's friend Simon Kenton left his mill and store in Springfield and took his fifteen-year-old son and went west. And how Zebulon Pike left St. Louis in August to explore the headwaters of the Mississippi River.

He got quiet and sad the day I told him these things. He spoke little. Soon he got up and left.

"He doesn't like to hear of white men pushing out the boundaries," Mama told me later. "Those things are for men to speak of. He doesn't wish to hear them from you."

"What does he wish to hear from me, then?"

"Talk about books. Learning. Let him read, as he's been doing. He likes the Bible and stories of Washington and Shakespeare."

So I left the men talk for my father and brothers to tell him. With the smoking of pipes and the serving of potato wine and my father's gentle and intelligent explanations, the men talk went well.

Tecumseh and I read Shakespeare, the Bible, and stories of Washington. I didn't like being unable to speak of other matters, but I did as Mama said.

Was he like James, then, always having to be right? Were all men the same?

They were. In the last week of his stay, we had a fight. We were reading Shakespeare one day when Moses jumped on my lap. Usually Moses stayed outside during the day, but it was raining and he wandered in.

"Cat." Tecumseh drew back.

"Yes. This is Moses. James brought him from Kentucky for me. He brought one for his Martha, too. We bred them and Moses is soon to be a father."

161

He was still scowling. "You name him after Chief Moses?"

"No. After the reverend with his white beard."

He did not see the humor. "Cats are bad."

"Bad?"

"My brother, the Prophet, tells us this. Some of our people have cats from the white man. Open Door says they are evil. Witches take the shape of cats."

"Moses is no witch. You don't believe in witches, do you?"

"Open Door believes in them. He says we must have the cats killed."

I held Moses close.

"And he says we must kill white man's dogs with the tails that wag when they are happy. They bring white man's evil to our villages."

I was taken aback. "Kill the dogs? Because they wag their tails?"

"We must only keep dogs whose tails do not wag. And who are never happy. But always watching."

"You mean wolves." I was horrified.

"Yes."

Mama was working in the kitchen. I knew she was listening, but she acted as if she were paying no mind.

"Shag has no evil in him," I argued. "And surely you're too intelligent to believe in witches."

"Open Door says we must kill witches and evil

162

amongst us. He says we must start with the dogs and cats."

"No! Our people did that back in Massachusetts years ago. Before we came to our senses. Now we know it is wrong. There are no witches! And you must tell your brother not to kill the dogs and cats."

He kept eyeing Moses, purring in my lap. "My brother is a prophet now. He must keep the people believing. For me to go against him is to weaken his power."

After that it was no good between us. He knew it, too. Again he got up and walked out. And this night he did not come back for supper. We saw woodsmoke out by his wigewa. He was eating alone. Daddy went out and spoke to him. They smoked their pipes under the stars.

When Daddy came back in he drew me aside. "Don't question his beliefs, Rebecca."

"He's wrong about witches. He's so intelligent. How can he believe in them just because his stupid brother says so?"

"I don't think he believes in them. But his brother does, and his brother is gaining power as a prophet and a spiritual leader. Tecumseh must keep the people believing in his brother. And in him. If it takes witches to do it, then there are witches."

"We can't let him have all their dogs and cats

killed, Daddy. Can't they find another way to keep the people believing in them?"

Daddy scowled and walked into the book room. He took a book down from the shelf and scanned it thoughtfully. "You have something there, Rebecca. And I think I have something here."

It was the *Kentucky Almanac*. He showed me the page.

It predicted an eclipse on the seventeeth of June, in the Year of Our Lord, eighteen hundred and six.

We stared at each other. My heart beat fast. "Do you want to show him this, Rebecca?" Daddy asked gently. "Or shall I?"

"You mean he could tell his people? Like a prophecy?"

Daddy nodded.

"Would it be right?"

"It would strengthen his power. Isn't it better to do it this way than through killing people as witches?"

And cats, I thought. And dogs because their tails wag when they are happy. I took the book from Daddy.

"Don't push," he told me. "The idea must be his. Not yours. You must only plant it in his mind and let it flower. Like you plant your rose bushes."

I went out into the clear October night to do some planting.

By the light of his fire, I showed him the book.

"This is certain?" he asked. "The black sun will come on this day?"

"Yes," I told him.

He nodded and fell silent, musing. Then he spoke. "My people are much fearful of eclipse."

"Yes," I said.

"It is a great sign from Weshemoneto."

"Yes," I said again.

"Thank you, Gal-o-weh girl. I am much in your debt. What can I give you for this knowledge you have given me?"

"Don't kill the dogs and cats," I said. "Tell your brother they are not witches. They are all God's creatures. But if he can't abide that, tell him to give them back to the white man."

He nodded slowly. "I will do this for you, Rebecca."

I knew a promise when I heard one. It was that and more. The more hung in the sweet darkness of the October night, all around us. I should leave, I minded. The more frightened me.

I took a few steps, then turned. "Can I ask you something, Mr. Tecumtha?"

"Yes."

"You're sad about Elizabeth, aren't you?"

He nodded yes.

"When you gave Mama the cold water root, you said the fever would be gone in five days. Was that a prophecy?"

"No. It was knowledge of the cold water root."

"She's going to die, isn't she?"

"Yes."

I knew a prophecy when I heard one, too.

But I did not know a gift. Or, more precisely, the meaning of it.

A week before he left he gave me the canoe. Apparently everyone in the family knew about it but me. It was made of bark, small and delicate, yet strong, with lovely curved lines.

After supper one night, he brought us all outside and presented it to me.

"For you, Gal-o-weh girl. I made it for you."

I clapped my hand over my mouth in delight and surprise. I had wanted my own canoe so badly! And now, here it was.

Everyone in my family was grinning at me. Even George, who had made the dowry chest instead of the canoe. I ran my hands over it lovingly.

"When did you make it?"

"In the woods. Every day."

"I thought you went to the woods to have visions."

He grew solemn and stood proud, arms folded across his middle. I could almost see the muscles in his arms through the deerhide shirt. The strength and dignity seeped out of him. Did no one else mind it but me?

"Oh, I didn't mean to *offend* you," I amended quickly. "I think canoes are much nicer than visions, anyway."

I was babbling.

He grinned. His white teeth flashed. George pushed me, and Mama looked from him to me and seemed perplexed. The electricity between me and Tecumseh was a living thing. I became embarrassed.

"Now you'll have to teach her to use the canoe, Tecumseh," John piped up.

"Oh, I wouldn't take up his time," I said. "George can teach me. Or Sam."

"I will teach," he said. "Like you taught me the proper way to speak. Like you taught me about Chief Michael, Chief Washington, and Chief Moses. And many other things. We start tomorrow, Gal-o-weh girl."

Nobody objected.

Surely, Elizabeth was dying. Mama and I went every evening to see her. We brought special teas and soups. Daddy sent for Dr. Drake, who came all the way from Marietta with his *Surgical Dictionary* and his patent medicines.

He had Bateman's drops, Godfrey's cordial, Anderson's ague pills, and Hamilton's worm-destroying lozenges.

Nothing worked. Daddy paid him in corn, rye, and pork. And he left, muttering that he worked on a cash-only basis.

Owen Davis's sister, the midwife, was better but still

not good enough. Mama and I were the worst for her, I think. Whenever Elizabeth saw us, she brightened and sat up in bed. I read to her. Mama neatened the place, prayed with her, and made plans with her for spring.

I sensed that our visits were a strain, that Elizabeth knew she would never see spring, that she couldn't wait for us to leave her be so she could lie back and die in peace and without all the attendant fuss.

I felt guilty for my joy in Tecumseh all the rest of that last week he was with us. Guilty because Elizabeth lay dying under the last warm rays of the October sun. While I drifted in the canoe down the Little Miami River, my eyes filled with the flaming color of the trees and underbrush and this masterful Indian chief who looked like the pictures of the Roman gods I'd seen in my daddy's books.

Everything about Tecumseh made my head addled. The graceful, sure moves of him, the sound of his voice as it echoed off the water, the thrust of his shoulders as he showed me the proper way to hold the paddle. I rushed through my chores and my studies and grew impatient with the clock for not chiming away the hours fast enough until I could be with him.

Then I'd lose myself in the world as he showed it to me from the canoe. He pointed out the tracks of animals, vegetation I'd never paid mind to, herbs that his people used as medicine, fall flowers.

One afternoon he showed me some sassafras trees. He knew how old they were by looking at them. And told me how his people got medicine from its roots. But first they gave a tobacco offering to the tree, thanked it, and promised to use its roots, leaves, and berries in the most respectful way.

I thought it very nice they thanked the trees. That was more than James did when I sewed a button on his shirt.

Then I had another thought. "Couldn't you get some medicine from it for Elizabeth?" I asked.

He shook his head no and gave me such a look that I knew that Elizabeth was going to die soon.

Another afternoon he told me how his people flavored their meats. "Different woods make different flavors," he said. "Hickory, maple, wild cherry."

It all seemed like a wealth of simple truths. But more important, I had the feeling he had told these things to no white before. That I was being honored.

In that week I learned to maneuver the bark canoe on the river. He taught me how to avoid the rocks, how to tell when the current was going to change, how to balance my weight.

By the end of the week I was rowing the canoe myself. But we'd only gone as far as the first bend in the river.

"Let's go to the second bend," I said.

He shook his head. "Enough for now. Come this far

every day while I am gone, until the first snow falls. Promise."

I promised.

He made me promise that I would not attempt to go to the second bend in the river until he returned in spring. It was too dangerous. I promised that, too. Although I was confident in my ability to do it. When I was with him I felt I could do anything.

But when it came time for him to take his leave from us, I could not seem to walk across a room without bumping into things.

He would not tell me where he was going when he left. And Daddy said not to ask him. I watched him packing up his things, and I knew he was off to do something very important.

It came to me then that he *was* important. He was an Indian chief, not only important but magnificent. Tribes were waiting for him to return, to hear him speak, to listen to his prophecies.

I hated them, every last man, woman, and child of them.

As I watched him making ready to leave, I knew that I was merely a little slip of a girl with whom he had dallied away his precious time. I felt cast aside before he was even gone.

Then he left us, and the world turned cold.

The snow came early. The trees creaked at night with the wind, and I lay awake seeing him on his horse making his way back to his people. Alone in the wind.

The fields and farm lay blanketed in misery. James came home, and he and George set a date for the hog killing. Sam saw to his beaver traps. John helped my father mend harnesses. I helped the boys make cider, did some weaving for Mama, and taught Ann, who was six now, to hem a shirt.

Before the snows came I walked down to the river. But I could not bring myself to put my canoe into the water without Tecumseh. I kept hearing his voice, seeing the things he'd pointed out to me.

I lost my appetite. I did not sleep right at night. There was an ache inside me I could not give a name to.

I put my canoe away and wished I had some of Bateman's drops or Anderson's ague pills.

Elizabeth died before Christmas.

CHAPTER 13

January–May 1806

Only James would have gotten married in the middle of January when the snows were high. Mama couldn't set her carpet on the ground for dancing, and it was nigh on to impossible to get from one place to another.

The wedding was held at Mr. Townsley's place. Everyone came. The house was fair to bursting. But all the children behaved. After all, Mr. Townsley was their teacher.

Even Will came to see his brother through. We had not seen hide nor hair of Will since Elizabeth's death. He stayed to himself, refusing all invitations to sup with us or attend church.

George stopped over to see him. Daddy stopped over to see him. Mama and I went. We found him lying on his unmade bed in his new house, which was strewn with every manner of debris. Dirty dishes were on the table. Dirty clothing on the floor. And there would be Will, just sitting on his bed and staring into the fire as if he, too, had an ague.

But he didn't. His brow was cool, his eyes were clear. Mama wept. "I didn't raise you like this, Will."

I think she would rather he had an ague.

"Like what, Mama?"

"To do nothing. To live in filth. I raised you up to arms and labor and a true Christian spirit."

"Leave me be, Mama" was all he would say.

As always when she was agitated, Mama resorted to Franklin. "After crosses and losses, men become humbler and wiser."

But I knew it wrung her heart to see Will like that.

James went to see him and came back more agitated than a housefly in August. Which was not difficult for James, even in January. "An ague of the mind," I heard him tell Mama. And then he resorted to being James. "If he doesn't come 'round soon, I'm going to beat the hell out of him."

I didn't know if James imparted these sentiments to Will on any of his visits. But Will came to the wedding. Sad and white in the face, speaking scarce a word, he came. But he came.

Daddy's old friend Simon Kenton came, too. He'd been in the Indian campaign with Daddy in '82. He'd been captured by Shawnees, by the British, by just about anyone who was doing capturing back in those days. The Shawnees had made him run a gauntlet in which he was near killed. Then they adopted him. He defended Boonesboro, Kentucky, against Indian attacks, arranged prisoner exchanges, was at the Greenville Treaty, and lost his wife, Martha.

He was married again. And he saw the sickness in Will.

"I've known that boy since he was a tyke in Kaintuck," I heard Kenton say to Daddy at our end of the table. "What ails him?"

"He lost his wife," Daddy said.

Kenton just grunted.

"He acts like he has no reason to live," Mama added.

"Somebody ought to tell him different," Kenton mumbled.

The dancing commenced. Unable to bear the festivity of it, Will got up and wandered outside. I slipped out shortly after. The night was clear and cold.

"Will?"

The farmyard was blanketed with snow. Overhead a full moon cast the light of day. Pine knot torches were set on fence posts. Will leaned against a fence rail, brooding. Oh, it was a heartbreak thing, this sickness that sat on him. I moved toward him.

"Go back inside, Rebecca."

"It's killing Mama and Daddy to see you like this, Will. And it'll kill you, if you don't come 'round. I heard Daddy say so."

"The sooner the better, then."

"No. Don't say that. You've so much to live for!"

"Like what?"

"Your farm."

"Devil take the farm."

"You've worked so hard on it."

"For Elizabeth. And she's gone."

"You have us. We need you, Will. Daddy said he was going to ask you to come home to live again. With James moving onto his own place, he could use the help."

"James. He has all the luck. Why does he have all the luck, Rebecca? Nothing bad ever happens to James."

"Hush," I said. "Plenty of people have bad luck."

"To lose a wife so young? Name me one hereabouts."

Simon Kenton, I thought. He was thirty-three when he'd married Martha, Daddy had told us. And she was seventeen. But I said nothing. "Mrs. Maxwell lost her baby."

"I've no heart for the farm," he said dully. "I've no heart for anything anymore."

"Oh, Will, I can't bear seeing you like this!"

"There's nothing more to wait for," he said.

I didn't know what to say. For weeks he wouldn't

speak to us. Now he was putting things into words I didn't want to hear. So I turned and ran back to the house.

Simon Kenton came out. He stood there, pulled off his fur cap. His blue eyes met mine.

I knew he had a deep gash in his skull and an ax scar on his collarbone from being captured by Indians.

I also knew the gash in his heart and the scar on his mind were deeper. But here he was, strong and alive as ever, a legendary Indian fighter and scout. We children had heard about him from my father all our lives.

"Miss Rebecca." He bowed to me.

I nodded. "Mr. Kenton."

I also knew how his first wife had died. Daddy had told us we were never to ask him about it, never to bring the matter up in Kenton's presence. "Or you'll answer to me," Daddy had said. "It's a heartbreak thing with that man. A heartbreak thing."

"Is your brother out here?"

"Yessir. He's brooding. Over by the fence."

In the light of the pine knot torch I saw the blue eyes sparkle. "I take it you're not much for brooding, Miss Rebecca," he said. His voice was deep and musical.

"No, sir."

"Neither am I."

"I'm worried for Will, Mr. Kenton. He says there's nothing more to wait for in life. He's only twenty-one."

He sighed and drew on his deerskin gloves. "Do you think he'd take a notion in his head that tomorrow morning is worth waiting for?"

"Sir?"

"Tomorrow I leave to go back west, Miss Rebecca. I asked your father. He said he'd miss Will a powerful lot, but he'd be glad for me to take him with me. I leave tomorrow morning."

"Oh, Mr. Kenton, would you really take him with you?"

"Do you think he'd want to go?"

"It's a chance for him, sir, to do something outside himself. But why should he listen to you? He won't listen to any of us."

"Indeed, why?"

I knew what I must do then. I must chance it. I must risk offending Mr. Kenton and angering Daddy. For Will.

"If you could tell him about yourself, sir."

"Myself?"

I blushed. "Yes. I know I shouldn't speak of it. My daddy told me that. How your wife died."

He scowled. I saw the pain cross his face, and his voice was not musical now. "What did your daddy tell you?"

"Oh, sir, I dasn't."

"But you did already, so go on."

I went on. "She was expecting her fifth. And wasn't

177

well. And you were away. So she had her servants bring her bed downstairs. Some burning piece of wood shot out of the fireplace upstairs and the room caught fire. Daddy said the upstairs floor caved in on Martha."

From inside the house came the sound of fiddle music, laughter. They would be stealing the bride about now. How ludicrous it all seemed. Will's bride was stolen, gone. So was Mr. Kenton's.

He spoke finally. "That's right, Rebecca. Except that she was terribly burned and the child stillborn. But if you know this, doesn't Will know it, too?"

"Will doesn't know anything now, sir. Except his own misery."

Simon Kenton put his hat on again, nodded, and walked past me.

I shouldn't have said it, I minded. I had no right. But he patted my shoulder in passing. And then I knew I'd done the right thing.

Next morning Will left with Simon Kenton to go west.

Funny, I thought. Daddy risked the farm to keep Sam here. And now he's risking losing Will in order to save him.

Would we ever see Will again? I didn't know.

Before they left in the morning, I sought out Simon Kenton. "You'll take good care of my brother, won't you?" I asked.

"Like he was mine," he promised.

"I feel responsible, in part, that he's going."

"You are. It worked, my telling him about Martha."

"I went against Daddy's wishes."

"How old are you now, Rebecca?"

"Fifteen in the fall."

"Martha was fourteen when I fell in love with her. Old enough to know her mind. Though we waited three years to keep her mother happy."

I felt better when he told me that. About a lot of things.

Will spoke to us more after he left us than he had in the weeks since Elizabeth had died. He wrote to us from all over.

In early March he wrote telling how he and Kenton saw Tecumseh's new village near Fort Greenville, on the western edge of Ohio. Though they hadn't presumed to enter the village and disturb things, they had spoken with white people who lived in Greenville.

"The Indian village has fifty cabins, many wigewas, and a great meetinghouse," Will wrote. "The citizens of Greenville are very agitated that it is here. All kinds of Indians pass through Greenville to get to the Indian village."

In late March he wrote how he and Kenton had come across a meeting of many Shawnees on the headwaters of the Great Miami River.

"They are calling it the Stony Creek Council," Will wrote. "I wanted to go inside. I reminded Kenton that I know Tecumseh. He said no and did some scouting. Well, it's a good thing I didn't go in. Kenton thinks it's a war council. He saw a post in the middle of the camp, and the Indians were throwing tomahawks at it. He saw black wampum belts being passed around."

Daddy was reading the letter at supper.

"War?" Mama said. "Impossible. Not Tecumseh."

"Black wampum belts mean war, Mama," Sam said.

I said nothing. Everybody was talking at once. Even John, who was twelve now and full of blood lust. And, of course, Andrew, who was ten, aped everything John did.

Ann smiled at me. It was not a nice smile. It was priggish. She was seven, the age I was when I met Tecumseh. She teased me about him. I'd smack her if I could. I would someday, soon. The only ones I could abide in my family those days were George and Anthony. But George was away, helping to build another courthouse. Anthony was too young to sass me at near two. He toddled about and needed love, great drafts of it, like Saxony needed great drafts of water after I'd ridden her.

Daddy recommended reading: "Simon and I (he allows me to call him Simon, Daddy) left the area and went forthwith to warn the settlers. We stopped at every cabin, all the way to Urbana. Then he took the east bank of the Mad River and I took the west, to do some more warning. I felt like Paul Revere. When we got to Springfield we found a lot of those settlers at the blockhouse there. We holed up with them for four days. But nothing happened except that Major Moore, who's in charge, wanted to go under a flag of truce to the Stony Creek Council.

"Then he decided we'd better tell the governor first. So he dispatched a letter that should be in the same mail run to Chillicothe as this."

It was. A rider brought a note around to Daddy from the governor that night.

Daddy left to meet with him and never came home until morning.

I heard him come in at first light. I'd tossed on my cornhusk mattress all night, dreaming half-dreams, wishing I could be with Kenton instead of Will. And wishing, at the same time, I'd never met Tecumseh.

A war council? Would he do that and betray us? Had all our friendship meant nothing to him? Was he, then, just a savage? Then toward dawn when I did sleep I had a terrible dream.

I was with Tecumseh in my bark canoe on the river. Then of a sudden he was gone and I took the canoe to the second bend.

There I saw dead bodies, hundreds of them, all white. Worse yet, I saw Tecumseh standing in the middle of the dead bodies. His eyes were shining, like those of the deer. Then I saw a white man raise his rifle and shoot Tecumseh. I saw him fall.

I awoke with a start, sweating and frightened, to hear Daddy's footsteps coming up the stairway.

I got up from my bed. Ann still slept in my room, but in her own bed on the other side now. I put a blanket around my shoulders and crept out into the hall.

From behind their closed door I heard Daddy talking.

"Govenor Tiffin wrote to Moore. He wrote that likely the Indians are preparing for war, but not against the whites. He's given permission for the party to go in and palaver with the Indians. He's sent a letter to the Indians themselves. I helped him compose it. He's sent a white wampum belt to go along with it."

"So he doesn't think there will be war?" Mama asked.

"No. But he urges our militia to be ready anyway. And for us to becalm the citizens of Chillicothe."

"I'll send Rebecca out on a few errands tomorrow," Mama said.

"Why don't you just let me ride and spread the word, Mama? Paul Revere never went with pies and jellies."

"You're doing the opposite of what he did," she reminded me. "You're going not to warn them but to tell them there is no danger. Yours is a friendly visit."

I fastened another sack of pies onto Saxony's saddle.

"Now be especially careful with the Turners," she called after me. "We can't have them leaving. Or others will follow. And remember, if passion drives, let reason hold the reins."

I might have known that she couldn't leave Ben Franklin out of it.

I rode and visited all day. The Gowdys, the McPhersons, the Quinns, the McCullys, the Andersons, and the Paxsons.

There I found Indian Joe packing up his blanket, buffalo robe, and fishing things. I slipped off Saxony's back.

"You're leaving? Old Baldy hasn't leafed out yet."

He grunted. "This spring I go early," he said.

"Why?"

"Bad feeling toward Indians."

"Have the Paxsons bad feeling for you?"

"Better go now" was all he would say.

I went into the house to deliver my huckleberry and peach jelly, my crab-apple pie, and the good word I'd given to everybody. There was nothing to fear. Governor Tiffin had sent in a white wampum belt. He had written to the Indians. He did not think they would war against us.

They said nothing about Indian Joe. I left and went to the Maxwells.

"What does Tiffin know?" Nancy Maxwell said to me. I'd saved her for last. Because, for the first time in my life, I dreaded visiting her.

"He's the governor," I said. "It's his job to know."

"He's a politician. Their job is to say what people want to hear," she told me.

I sat sipping tea. How much could I tell her? She was my dearest friend. Could I trust her? "Tecumseh wouldn't make war against us," I said finally.

Nancy Maxwell looked at me. And I at her. I hadn't wanted it to come to this.

"Rebecca," she said sadly, "you're smitten with him, child."

I did not deny it. And it felt good to have it out before someone.

"It's all right. He's handsome and strong. You'll get over it."

"I don't want to get over it," I said.

"You're young. Only fourteen."

"Fifteen in October."

"Too young."

"Simon Kenton fell in love with his Martha when she was fourteen. She returned the love. They waited three years to marry to please her mother."

"Oh, Rebecca! What are we going to do?"

We were not talking about the Indians making war on the whites now. And we both knew it.

"I almost pray they make war," Nancy Maxwell said. "So you will see."

"See what?" I asked.

"What you cannot see *until* they make war. And which I pray you see before then. For I am certain they soon will."

It sounded like a riddle. Which in fact it was. My whole life was a riddle right then. And only Nancy Maxwell knew it.

It was all right between us, though. Nothing changed. In spite of what I'd admitted to her. Or not denied. We drank our tea and ate Mama's crab-apple pie. When I left, she hugged me. "I'll not tell anyone," she promised. "You can count on me. And come and talk whenever you have need."

I hugged her and left. I did not like being Paul Revere, I decided. Even if I was doing it backwards.

Only one family left in fear of an Indian attack. The Turners. And in spite of Mama's apprehensions, no one else followed.

Another letter came from Will in February. Sometimes I thought it was better when he was not talking to us. This one told of how he'd gone to the Shawnee council with Kenton and Major Moore.

"Tecumseh met us. He gave no sign that he knew me. It was all very official. But he sent us away, assuring us they would not attack any white settlement. And that Tiffin will receive a letter from him in one moon."

Our militia started to drill, and we awaited the letter.

In one moon it came. Daddy and James went together to the governor's house. They brought it home so we could see it.

It was very long. In it Tecumseh promised friendship and love between the Indians and whites.

"We were entirely innocent," he wrote. "Of what the white people wanted to impute on our nation, was absolutely out of our knowledge."

And: "We have immediately return our prayers to the Great Spirit above, for you and will never forgotten your goodness towards us and we thanks him for having given us such a good and wise man."

"What's wrong, Rebecca?" Mama asked. "Aren't you happy? There will be no war!"

I nodded yes. But tears were in my eyes. "His English is terrible," I said. "I taught him better than that. He knows to say *never forget*, not *never forgotten*." I ran from the room.

"No matter how he says it," James called after me, "he remembers. And that's all that matters."

* * *

It was not all that mattered to me. My pride was injured. I knew I'd taught Tecumseh better than that. How could he write such a garbled letter to the governor! Ann wrote better!

Things quieted down. Then at the end of April came another letter from Will. This news was worse than the last.

"I write from Indiana territory. Some Delawares, who are disciples of Open Door, Tecumseh's brother, charged some fellow Indians with being witches, summoned Open Door to their village to judge them, and have executed them."

A terrible fear gripped my innards. Could Tecumseh now say *I will never forgotten* what we spoke of?

"They tortured and burned one old woman named Ann Charity," Daddy read on. "She was converted by the Moravian missionaries. Then they executed Twisting Vines, an aged Delaware chief, also a Christian. Then an old man named Joshua who'd been a carpenter for the Moravians."

Again Daddy was reading the letter at supper.

"Where was Tecumseh?" I could scarce speak.

Daddy scanned the letter. "At Stony Creek," he said. "Will writes Tecumseh knew nothing of the witch burnings. And he says that he and Simon Kenton personally informed Governor Harrison of the matter. Harrison has sent a letter to the Delawares saying that Open Door is an imposter. And telling them they should demand proof from him that he is a messenger of the Deity."

"Open Door *is* an imposter!" I said. I minded the day Tecumseh had sat reading with me and we talked about the dogs and the cats and how he needed his brother to have power. The day Daddy had taken the *Kentucky Almanac* off the shelf and I'd gone out to show the date of the next eclipse to Tecumseh.

Daddy minded it, too. I saw the look on his face.

Proof? My eyes met Daddy's. And I knew what he was thinking.

As spring came I wished Will would come home, go back to his farm, sit on his unmade bed, and stare into the fire again. I wished I'd never encouraged Simon Kenton to tell him about Martha.

Each time a letter came from him, I was afraid to listen when Daddy read it.

In May another letter came. This time the news was heartening.

"The Indians are giving back all their dogs and cats to the white people," Will wrote. "Everywhere we go, the whites tell us that Indians are approaching their farms under a sign of truce and leaving off dogs and cats."

I squeezed my eyes shut tight and felt the tears in my throat when Daddy read that. *Will never forgotten.*

"The witch hunts have stopped," Will wrote. "What we hear is that the Delawares visited Tecumseh and his brother at their Greenville village. They demanded proof that Tecumseh's brother is a prophet. Open Door gave them a sign. We do not know what it is, but the witch hunts have stopped. And I will be home soon to help with spring planting."

I should have been happy when I went to bed that night. Tecumseh had stopped his brother from burning people as witches. He'd kept his word to me about the dogs and cats. Will would soon be home, his old self again.

So, then, what was wrong? This: I knew what the sign was that the Prophet had given. It had not come from the Deity. It had come from the *Kentucky Almanac*.

CHAPTER 14

May–June 1806

I woke up the next morning to see a blanket of snow on the ground. And more falling. Snow the first week in May was not unusual for us. What happened with the snow was.

Indian Joe came home. Gone only five weeks and he'd come home four days ago, sick. Mrs. Paxson sent a note around. "With all the confusion about Indian attacks, I've been too busy to contact you," she wrote. "I am so sorry. He asked for Rebecca. I was going to send for her this morning."

Indian Joe had died the night before. Of pneumonia.

"What Indian attacks?" I was near to tears. "The only Indian she needed to worry about was him. And she didn't."

"Hush, Rebecca," Daddy said sternly. "The Paxsons took care of Indian Joe for years."

I hushed.

"We will hold his funeral tomorrow. Reverend Armstrong will preside, and we wish you all to come," Daddy continued reading.

I stood up. "No funeral. Not the way they want. Indian Joe told me how he wants to be buried."

"Have you taken leave of your senses, Rebecca?" Daddy asked.

"No, sir. I'm speaking my mind." I knew Daddy held with such.

"You've been doing a powerful lot of that lately."

We were at breakfast. With the snow belaboring things and James having ridden over, it was almost festive. And we lingered.

James and Martha were living with her father until their fine new brick house was built, west of the Fairfield Pike. This morning he'd come to consult about it with Daddy.

"What did Indian Joe tell you?" Mama asked.

So I related to them his wishes. Then I waited for James to laugh. He didn't.

"Old Mr. Paxson will never allow that," Sam said. "After all these years, he'll want to bury Indian Joe properlike."

"This is properlike. For him. Daddy, please, you've got to do something," I begged.

191

"I have tax assessor business today, Rebecca," he said. "And the boys have their planting."

"In the snow?"

"It will stop by noon. My neck doesn't hurt. The sun will shine soon."

"Then I'll ride over myself and talk to the Paxsons."

It was then that James stood up. "I'll ride over with you, Rebecca."

I stared at him, not believing. James? Who was always too busy with his surveys and now with his new house? James?

Yes, James. Who had the respect of everyone in Chillicothe. As much as Daddy. Maybe more now that he had his fancy surveying job. James who was going to be a daddy himself in November. Well.

James not only stood with me when I told the Paxsons what Indian Joe had made me promise. He said he'd stand by them if anyone criticized what they did.

Then he said, "We ought to do it today. Now. I'll help."

Well, the Paxsons were so flustered at having the county surveyor, held in such high esteem, offer his services, busy person that he was, that they agreed.

Or it could have been because they felt guilty allowing Indian Joe to go off so early in the cold. Before Old Baldy leafed out. I like to think it was a little bit of both.

James helped Mr. Paxson wrap Indian Joe in his buffalo robe and blanket. Then they put him on Mr. Paxson's sled.

I gathered his things, his fishing line, his hooks, some bacon, and bread. I wrapped the bacon and bread in burlap and put them beside him on the sled.

Then we walked to the small grove on the east side of the Paxson farm, to Old Baldy, and I looked up in surprise.

"It wasn't leafed out yesterday," Mrs. Paxson said.

I will say one thing for her. She stood with me and waited while James and Mr. Paxson dug the grave. The snow had stopped, as Daddy had predicted. The ground was not frozen. In no time at all they had a nice grave dug for him.

We buried him there, under Old Baldy, where he used to sit and tan his skins.

"Rebecca, you ought to say some words," James directed.

I thrust about in my mind for what to say. Then I started. "Indian Joe, Old Baldy has put out his leaves for you. They're as big as a squirrel's ear. It'll be nice and shady for you here in the summer. And in the winter Old Baldy will keep his branches over you and protect you. I've sent along your fishing things and some bread and bacon. There isn't a house here in Chillicothe where the lady doesn't have one of your baskets. James's Martha has two. So we're all going to think of you now and then. And we hope you'll think of us. And remember us to Moneto. Indian Joe, speaking for myself, *I will never forgotten you.*"

The Paxsons stared at me. James didn't. He smiled.

I swore, I would never say another word against James as long as I lived.

The seventeenth of June was very hot and still. Katydids sang steadily. Mama and I finished our morning chores and took the noon meal for the menfolk out under the pear trees in back. Cold meat, cheese, deviled eggs, tomatoes, and baked apples.

Anthony was running around after a kitten fathered by Moses. Martha had given it to us.

Ann had stayed with Martha and James overnight. Andrew and John were in the fields with Daddy.

No one said anything at breakfast. It was as if everyone had forgotten. I prayed they had.

I had not. I'd been nervous as a skunk out in daylight all morning. In the kitchen I'd dropped a dish of peach preserves, nicked my finger while scraping potatoes, and near forgot to take the baked apples out of the beehive oven.

I'd been waiting. As I was now. The heat and stillness seemed to sit on my shoulders as I sat and sewed.

Mama was on me to start stitching a dowry. What for? Who would I wed? "I don't see any young Simon

194

Kenton riding down the trace in my direction," I told her.

So I was stitching a baby dress for James and Martha's little one. Finally I could bear the waiting no longer.

"Do you think it will happen, Mama?" I asked.

"If it serves the Lord's purposes."

"Why would it serve His purposes? And how?"

She shrugged. "It is not for us to question, Rebecca."

Why, I wanted to say. Why not question?

And then it happened.

Slowly, the sun that had been climbing so steadily in the heavens all morning was getting a shadow over it.

That shadow seemed to walk across the hills in the distance, then across our corn and wheat fields. Within a matter of minutes, it grew darker and darker.

"Mama," I whispered.

A flock of crows in the cornfield took flight and disappeared into the trees. Shag whimpered and came to lay by my feet. I heard our cows mooing in distress.

Mama kept right on with her sewing.

It got darker and darker, like dusk after the sun disappeared behind the hills. I looked up.

I could see stars.

Anthony came running over to me, dragging his small blanket. "Night-night," he said.

I gathered him in my arms and cuddled him close. The kitten jumped into my lap, too. From inside the house I could hear Daddy's clock striking. Twelve noon.

Mama set down her sewing. "Oh dear, we should have brought out candles. I can't see the hem anymore," she said.

In the distance I heard the menfolk coming from the fields. I heard John and Andrew shouting. "The eclipse! The eclipse!"

I held Anthony close. I could see. Clearly.

I could see Tecumseh somewhere, in one of his villages, stepping outside his wigewa and holding up his arms. I could see his brother, Open Door, beside him. Exultant. And shouting, "You see? I am a prophet, people. Now will you believe me?"

The eclipse served a purpose, all right. And it wasn't God's. I decided that right there and then. I didn't care what Mama said.

CHAPTER 15

Spring 1807

I don't know why, but just because spring had come and the woods were budding, the barrens green again, and the clouds drifted high in blue skies over the sun-kissed hills, everyone had the notion that I ought to go courting.

I was near sixteen, taller than Mama. I had a bosom more than respectable, I could do a reel and jig with the best when we had our dances, and for all intents and purposes I'd stopped being a hoyden. Even James said so.

So everyone presumed it was time for me to cast an eye about and see who I would wed.

I didn't. Oh, I liked Bushrod Sheley well enough. And I saw his aunt Nancy Maxwell's face smile in tenderness when he asked me to walk out with him. I did it to please her. She was my friend. Bushrod was her sister's boy, up from Springfield where Simon Kenton had his mill and trading post.

Bushrod brought a wagonload of items from the post to Chillicothe — furs, skins, ginseng root, cranberries all gotten from the Shawnees. We needed these things like we need more trees, but he had to have an excuse for the trip, I suppose. He worked, after a fashion, for Kenton.

He adored Kenton and wanted to be like him. The only problem, he said, was that there were no wars right now. More's the pity, I supposed.

He thought he adored me, too. In the fortnight he'd stayed with the Maxwells I'd suffered all kinds of manifestations of his adoration. He'd been over five times to sup. We'd gone to three frolics. And he'd given me a gift, a brand-new copy of *The Compendious Dictionary of the English Language* by Noah Webster.

This last I did not consider suffering. We finally had a dictionary in this country.

"Embrace is spelled with an *e* not an *i*," he said. And he pointed it out to me.

All of this — the gift, the frolics, his cheek — was the fault of my brothers. And Aaron Burr.

My brothers met Bushrod earlier this year when the Ohio militia was called out to put down an attempt by

Burr to set up his own little western empire on Blennerhassett Island on the Ohio River.

Mama said, "In heaven's name isn't it enough that Burr killed Alexander Hamilton?" Daddy said, "Thank heaven it happened before planting season." My brothers said little. They were glad enough to go, I thought. Winter bored them.

And so they met Bushrod, who boasted around the campfire one night how he worked for Simon Kenton winters and who his aunt was.

My brothers boasted about me. And invited him to Chillicothe. Talk about setting up empires! Men do it not only with land, it seems, but with women.

I baked Muster Day gingerbread for militia practice, just like they did in the old states. Every able-bodied man between eighteen and forty-five turned out ready to take on any comers. Our county formed one regiment. General Worthington was in charge. James was a major.

I didn't know who Bushrod thought *he* was, but he wore himself out marching, firing his musket, and doing mock maneuvers. Was I supposed to be taken with such displays of bravery? I was not.

Of course, he was the first one to show up for the picnic Mama, I, and the other women had prepared.

I heaped his plate with ham, beef, fowl, potatoes, cabbage.

"Will you set and eat with me, Rebecca?"

He was very tall. His hair was red and his eyes blue. If I lived in another place and another time, I would have been glad to not only set and eat with him, but do all other manner of things people do when courting. Just because I hadn't done them didn't mean I didn't know what they were.

As it was, for this time and place he was the handsomest, most polite, and agreeable man who had ever asked me to set and eat with him. I did not wish to hurt him. So I said yes.

I'd had the misfortune to be holding six-month-old Richard, James and Martha's baby, at the time. He'd just whimpered in his cradle under the tree and I picked him up, then handed him over to Martha.

I did not miss the look on Bushrod's face when he saw me cuddling Richard.

"You like children?"

"What a silly question!" We took our plates and found a place to sit.

"Why is it silly?"

"I've been caring for little ones all my life. Right now Anthony prefers me to Mama."

"You don't look like anybody's mama. You're a right pretty girl, Rebecca."

"I told you the other night when we walked out not to say things like that."

"Why? Don't you like me?"

"Because I do like you. And I'd like to be friends. But I can't be if you go and speak such foolishment."

"James said you were different from most girls your age."

"I certainly hope I am."

"Not too much, I hope. What would you do if I kissed you?"

"I'd tell your aunt. And she'd draw a bead on you like she did on those Indians."

He laughed good-naturedly. He had dimples. A lock of hair fell over his forehead. Curly hair.

I wished, for the hundredth time, that I was not smitten with Tecumseh. He had ruined my notion of men for all time.

Then Bushrod got serious. "We're going to have war soon, you know."

I said I didn't.

"If not with the Indians then with the British."

"You sound as if it makes no never-mind to you who it's with."

I was being sassy. He paid no mind. "Over in Springfield, Griffith Foos is making a fort out of his home. Lots of people are scared."

"Of what?"

He leaned closer. "The British are moving among the Indians. Inciting them to fight against the Americans. People are wary. There's no end to the number of Indians trekking to Greenville to hear Tecumseh speechify. They say he has eight hundred Indians with him. Especially now, after that business where his brother predicted the eclipse. People have been writing to the governor. They want Tecumseh out of Greenville. He doesn't belong there. It's American land, according to Wayne's treaty."

I said nothing. Not for lack of words. But because my mouth wouldn't work.

"How well do you know Simon Kenton?" he asked.

"He's a friend of ours." I had to clear my throat in order to speak.

"He's a good fighter. When war comes, I want to be in any scouting party he leads. He says we have to kill Tecumseh. Because he's getting too much power. And if we let him live, he's going to raise the Devil all over the Northwest."

Was he being stupid, this Bushrod person? Or just downright mean? Didn't he know Tecumseh was a friend of our family? Hadn't my brothers told him? I felt bile rising in my throat. I put my plate aside.

"Simon Kenton would never say that."

"Well, he has. I heard it with my own ears."

"Your ears need boxing." I stood up.

He stared up at me. "Now what did I *say*, Rebecca?"

"If you don't know, I won't tell you." I looked around in confusion. It wasn't true. Simon Kenton *hadn't* said it. Had he? All around me people were sitting or standing in groups, holding plates, talking, joking, laughing. I wanted to run, but I had no excuse. At near sixteen you just don't run in the middle of a social without a reason.

"Rebecca, Rebecca, come quick. They're going to have footraces! I'm going to run. Come run with me!"

Ann came flying across the grass toward me. Little Anthony toddled after her. I was never so glad to see Ann in my life.

I ran in the footrace with her. Two days later, Bushrod went back to Springfield. I did not see him before he left. So much for courting. I thought I would stay an old maid.

I had a score to settle now with Simon Kenton. Kill Tecumseh, indeed. I didn't care if he does have a hollow in his head from a Shawnee tomahawk. He should have known better.

I wasn't too happy with Tecumseh, either. Oh, I knew I bartered that information about the eclipse in exchange for his promise not to kill the dogs and cats. But I saw the power his fool brother had gained from it, and I was concerned.

I told no one of my concerns. Spring was a busy enough time without raising a ruckus because of my personal affronts. Especially that year when Daddy was having our new house built.

It was made of stone. Mama said it will have more

rooms than we need now that James was gone and George traveled around so much. But Will was back. He sold his farm to Reverend Armstrong and had come home to help Daddy. I was tempted to ask Will about Simon Kenton. But I thought not. He went about his business quietly and at peace with himself at long last. He worked and read and helped with the new house, and the little ones loved having him around. He was even raising a prize steer to exhibit at the next Fourth of July celebration.

No. I would just have to muddle through myself. And wait.

CHAPTER 16

June 1807

A *man came* to Chillicothe claiming he had a marvel. We were not immune to marvels. Certainly, after a spring of trying to keep the weeds and rabbits out of the kitchen garden, weaving a cloth for the table James was making for our new house, minding baby Anthony, who was three, paddling my canoe, and teaching Ann to spell by the new *Webster's*, which they do not yet have in her school, I was ready for a marvel.

This one was a pig. It went by the name of Claudia. The man went by the name of Ebenezer Hartsook. He said he was a mason by trade until he discovered his pig could read and write and spell ordinary Christian names.

So he gave up masonry to travel the country with her. He charged five cents for admittance to this marvel. And Ann and Anthony had been begging me to take them to see it.

Finally, the last week in June I relented. Or rather, Daddy did, and gave us the money. I think the only reason was that word came to us this week that the British man-o'-war *Leopard* fired on our frigate *Chesapeake*. We also heard they seized four of our men whom they claim are British deserters. Daddy got so mooded up over that he said, "Go take the little ones and have a good time."

"How dare those redcoats do that?" I asked Mama.

"We don't call them redcoats anymore," she said. "That's from the last war."

"Well, they may have changed the color of their coats, but they haven't changed themselves any."

"The wolf sheds his coat once a year," Mama said. "His disposition never."

Franklin. So, she was beset, too. And why not? James is a major in the militia. Sam, Will, and George would go, too, if war came.

Hartsook had the pig set up in a tent in front of Gowdy's Mercantile. People were gathered around waiting to see her.

Never one to let fortune pass him by, Gowdy had a lemonade stand set up in the June heat. After half an hour's wait and three lemonades, we finally got in to see Claudia.

Well, our pigs could do what she did, too, I thought, seeing how Hartsook had her right foot all rigged up with some kind of a pulley that he operated from behind a curtain.

The pig was tame, to be sure. And clean. She even had a ribbon around her neck. And when Ann gave her name she did write it on a piece of slate. After a fashion. Only thing I couldn't figure was how he kept that chalk tied to her foot.

I was disappointed. And then angry. Not at Hartsook, at myself. Had I really thought I would see a pig who could write? And not a man who was clever enough to outwit the public?

Ann and Anthony loved it, though. And I hadn't the heart to tell them Hartsook was pulling her foot from behind that curtain. Time enough for them to learn we can't believe in some people or some pigs. No matter how much we want to.

Our house was full of old soldiers, those who had fought in the war with Daddy.

They had come to see Tecumseh.

He was there when Ann and Anthony and I returned from town. Word of his arrival had traveled. On the June wind. In the cry of the red-tailed hawk that I'd seen circling over our house. In the bluebird's ditty. It was passed, throat to throat, in the croaking of the frogs on the edge of the river.

Tecumseh had come.

Half a dozen horses were hitched in front of our house. Inside Mama was scurrying about, making ready for supper. Ann and I set to helping.

There was laughter, pipe smoking, jug passing, men talk from under the pear trees out back. Tecumseh was in the middle of it in the guest chair. If he saw me come in, he gave no sign.

I stole glances at him as I passed back and forth, carrying plates and cups outside to the trestle tables Sam and Will were setting up.

General Worthington was here. He'd given his elegant seat of a house a name now. Adena. Owen Davis, Mr. Townsley, James, Matthew Quinn, Mr. Maxwell, and Adam McPherson were here, too.

Then Mama called the men to the tables. My brothers sat with them. Even John and Andrew.

"Men talk." Mama smiled at me. "Let them get their fill. You and I and Anthony will eat here, where it's nice and quiet."

I didn't want to be nice and quiet. I wanted to shout and scream. My blood was pounding so loud it sounded in my ears. I hated being a girl just then. I wanted to be a man. But if I *were* a man, my blood wouldn't be pounding. It made no sense.

208

We ate. And every time they needed something outside I jumped up, telling Mama to sit, she was tired. I wanted to bring things to the table. I wanted to just walk by him. To watch him move. To see if the way he held his head was the way I remembered.

It was.

Of course, I listened to snatches of conversation. What had these men to discuss that I couldn't discuss? Fort Greenville? Governor Harrison? Vincennes? Black Hoof? Major Moore? I knew about all of it.

Dusk came. I sent Mama and Ann to bed and cleaned up. I put Anthony to bed. I could not be still. I swept out the book room. I would have swept out the whole farmyard if it wouldn't have looked foolish.

The sky in the west went red, pink, then purple. I looked at the sunset as if I'd never seen it before.

My brothers saw to the stock. Birds made going-to-sleep sounds. June bugs lighted up the darkness. Evening settled in. The men lighted lanterns outside.

Coffee. They would want more. Men always did. I brought out a fresh pot, set it on the table, and caught Tecumseh's eye. He nodded and smiled.

I felt myself dying. The feeling was beautiful.

Everyone seemed to be talking all at once, oblivious of the magic all around, the air that was sweet as Daddy's elderberry wine. I felt besotted with it.

I went into the house and lay on my bed. He isn't listening to them, I told myself. Because they're all talking at once. With the Shawnees, only one person speaks at a time and the others wait and listen. They don't know this because they don't know him. I do. Only I do.

The next morning I thought I'd dreamed him. He was something a person would dream. I got up and crept downstairs. Mama was setting bread in the oven. I started to make coffee. "Will they be back again today?"

"Not directly. They've all got farms."

"Well, I'm going with him in my canoe. Before they get to him again. Can't I, Mama? Please?"

She smiled. "Finish your chores first," she said.

I couldn't believe he was here, walking next to me. He was so tall! His shoulders so broad. His movements so sure as he carried the canoe to the riverbank. Yet it was all right, like I'd dreamed it would be. No verbal dueling between us, as I'd had to do with Bushrod Sheley, as all girls my age did with young men.

We set the canoe in the water at our pier, which is a great sycamore whose roots reach into the river. He smiled. He held it as I got in. He gestured I should sit. *We understood each other without talking.*

He paddled in silence for a bit and we drifted, enjoying the peace, the greenery, the sound of the water, the birdsong.

Then I spoke. "I've not taken it to the second bend. Can we go this morning?"

He nodded yes and handed me the paddle.

I took it and guided the canoe midstream. I went with the current, as he'd taught me. He leaned back and let the warm sun play on his face.

"Did my daddy's friends all satisfy themselves that you aren't going to make war on us?" I asked.

He waved the thought of them aside with a careless gesture. "No."

"Tecumtha, people are frightened that you are."

He said nothing.

"I must ask you something. And tell you something."

"Ask," he said.

"Did you tell your brother of the prediction in the almanac? Is that how he made his prophecy?"

He smiled sheepishly and nodded his head.

"And so your brother has much power now. The people think he is a prophet."

He sat forward and looked at his hands in his lap. I could see he was troubled. "I am much ashamed of this," he said. "It was deceit. My sister, Tecumapese, told me it was deceit. She scolded me. But I needed the people to believe in my brother. And in me. Now you scold, too."

He looked shamefaced. My heart melted.

"Tecumtha, I knew when I gave you the book about

the eclipse that you would tell your brother and it would give him power. I did it for that purpose. I wanted him to take his power from this and not from burning people as witches. Or killing dogs and cats. So the fault is mine as well as yours."

He nodded and eyed me shyly. "You don't tell anyone this, Gal-o-weh girl?"

"Of course not. But there *is* something I'm going to take you to task about." I said it severely. "Your letter to Governor Tiffin. Tecumtha, I taught you better English than that!"

"I did not get all the these-those words right?"

"Yes. But you said *Will never forgotten.* You should have said *forget.* It's the past tense. Don't you recollect when I taught you about tenses?"

He nodded slowly.

Such intelligence in those eyes, I minded. Such warmth! Such sincerity.

"I speak much better than I write." He grinned. "You see? I don't say better much anymore."

I nodded. My heart was going to break in two any minute now, I decided.

"I would make amends," he said. He was filled with a sober determination. He held out his hand for the paddle.

I handed it over and settled back. We were coming to the second bend in the river. The rapids were strong here, he'd been right. He guided the small canoe expertly through them, while I held on. Then, just past them, he paddled to the bank, into a little cove, stepped out, secured the canoe and held his hand out to me.

"Come."

I took his hand. It was warm and firm. He helped me up the bank and along a path. The sun shone down on us like a blessing. Birds sang. Wildflowers bloomed all around. I felt, just for a moment, that we were the only two people on the face of the earth as he gripped my hand in his.

This is how Adam and Eve must have felt, I decided.

After we went a little ways on the path he stopped. "Look." He was pointing at a small tree with some lovely white blossoms.

"They're lovely," I said.

"No." He dropped my hand and scowled. Then he picked some of the blossoms. "This is why I make you promise not to come to the second bend in the river. This tree, these flowers, must not be touched, not be taken. And I know how you look kindly on flowers."

I was puzzled. "What are they?"

He gestured to a log. "Sit."

I sat.

"I tell you this now, though it has never been told to any white person. I give you this secret to keep close to your heart always. In gratefulness for the secret you keep of the eclipse. You will tell no one of what I am about to say?"

I nodded and waited. My heart was hammering. I felt time and eternity pressing down on me.

"This tree and flower make Indians' secret. We suffer pain when torn by the lance, when pierced by the bullet, when burned, just as Shemanese do. But when we feel pain, we take the powder made from this blossom. We take it into battle with us. It makes still the pain."

"Like opium?" I asked.

"Much better."

I nodded, taken with the enormity of it. Then I had a question. "Would it have helped Elizabeth?"

"No. It does not cure disease. It only stills pain."

"This is a great secret, Tecumtha."

He nodded. "When the Indian loves, he speaks the truth; but if he does not, he is silent."

My mouth fell open. I could hear my heart thudding in my ears. *Had he just said he loved me?*

Then he stood up and took his tomahawk out of his belt. "Now I will kill the tree."

"No! Why? Why must you do that? I promised I wouldn't tell anyone! Don't you believe me?"

He smiled at me sadly. "I believe you. But I must make a pact of peace now. There are no other trees like this around. I have been much in the woods here on past visits. I know. So if I destroy this one, it makes a promise. It means you will never have need of it from us."

I stared at him. He started to chop away with his tomahawk. I stood watching, pondering his words.

It means you will never have need of it from us.

The act of tearing down the tree was his pact of peace.

I stepped aside and waited, humbled and moved, while he worked. When he finished, he put the toma-hawk back in place and held out his hand.

"Come, Gal-o-weh girl. We go back to your home now. No matter what they say of me, these soldier friends of your father, remember you and your family will never need this tree from us. Remember what you have seen here at the second bend of the river."

I took his hand. "I will never forgotten," I said.

CHAPTER 17

September 1807

Had he said he loved me?

All summer the question sat on my shoulders like a heavy cloak. It throbbed in my ears, reaching a frenzy in the August heat, like the sound of the katydids. It bled from my finger when I cut my hand slicing peaches to help Mama make preserves. It buoyed me up when I felt I would die from missing him.

I thought I came down with a fever. Mama felt my forehead and said no, I was cool. But she gave me some cold water root tea anyway. It did not help. There was something burning in me that I could not put out.

I took to going to the river to bathe in the heat of the afternoon when the men were in the fields and

Mama and Anthony napped. Sometimes I took Ann with me into the cool water and taught her to swim, as George had taught me.

Sometimes I stole off alone in my canoe. Three times that August I went to the second bend in the river, got out of my canoe, and stood looking at the cut-up remains of the tree. Just to assure myself it had all really happened.

I was there, looking at the remains of that tree and thinking of Tecumseh's promise that no harm would come to us the day we heard about the settler named Myer who was scalped and killed near Springfield.

Settlers near Springfield were in a panic. Some were sending wives and children back to Kentucky. Word spread on the hot September wind. Like a wildfire that could not be put out.

Some said Tecumseh had killed Myer. Some said Black Hoof was responsible. People hereabouts knew little about Indians for all their talk. So they spoke lies and they spoke rumors. They even sometimes spoke a little bit of the truth. One thing they said I knew to be true: Black Hoof and Tecumseh had had a falling-out. I thought Black Hoof had Myer killed to make it look bad for Tecumseh.

At three, Anthony was already a little man. With the exception of the few times he'd taken sick or been punished and run to me for coddling, I didn't think he'd ever been a baby. With six older brothers, how could he have been? He swaggered like James, swung a little wooden hammer like George, wrestled with Will, fed the dogs right along with Sam, helped with the hoeing like John, and tried to whistle like Andrew.

He didn't know he was so small. I mourned his lost babyhood. But loved him because he was so brave. He was a handsome little tyke, too. And he lisped. "I'm gonna thoot you," he'd say, aiming the little wooden rifle George carved for him. George also carved a small tomahawk for him that he stuck in his belt and was learning to throw.

He had the tomahawk the day I took him to town to do errands for Mama. The day I had high words with my dear friend, Nancy Maxwell.

I'd promised Anthony lemon drops, and Gowdy's Mercantile carried them. Nancy was in the store, chatting with two other ladies.

She introduced the other ladies as friends "visiting from Springfield." I knew that meant they had fled from the panic. She introduced me as her student, who played the pianoforte and recited Shakespeare.

I handed over the pennies for Anthony's lemon drops. Mr. Gowdy squatted down to put them in Anthony's hand. "Well, little fellow, and what's that tomahawk you've got there?" he asked.

Anthony pulled it out, made a stance as he'd learned from George, and posed ready to throw it.

I heard Nancy Maxwell gasp. Her face was white. "Surely you aren't allowing him to play with tomahawks, Rebecca?"

"George made it for him."

"He's learning to play like an Indian?"

"He's just a child, Nancy."

"My dear, child or no child, with the scalping of Myer by Tecumseh, it isn't proper. People won't know which way to take it."

I felt my blood coming to a boil. Why do they have to take it any way, I wanted to ask. And why do you assume Tecumseh killed Myer? But I didn't say it. After all, this was my dear friend Nancy.

Then Anthony did something only Anthony would do. He threw the tomahawk down the aisle of Gowdy's Mercantile with an Indian yelp. Just like George had taught him.

The two ladies from Springfield screeched. The way ladies from Springfield should never do because they should know better.

"Rebecca," Nancy said, "contain your little brother."

I recognized the tone as one she used when I hadn't practiced my music.

When I did not move immediately, she did. She grabbed Anthony and scolded gently. "Sweetheart, nice little boys don't play like murderous Indians."

"My name isn't sweetheart, it's Anthony," my brother said. "And I'm not nice. I'm Chief Anthony."

"For shame, Anthony." Then Nancy turned to me. "Does your mama know what a little ruffian he is? Haven't you taught him about the murderous Indians?"

The line was drawn then, between my friend Nancy and my little brother. I knew I had to take one side or the other. I chose Anthony.

"He isn't a ruffian. He's a little boy. And we don't teach him the Indians are murderous."

"But, child, they are," one of the Springfield ladies put in. "Why, Tecumseh is spiriting up his people to murder us all."

"Tecumseh didn't kill Myer," I told her.

"How can you say that?" the other Springfield lady asked.

"Her head is addled where Tecumseh is concerned," Nancy explained. "Poor dear child." She looked at me with real pity.

I looked at her with hatred I didn't know I had in me. "I'm not a child. And my head has never been more clear. Tecumseh didn't kill Myer. And if Anthony wants to play with tomahawks, I'll not stop him. My brothers throw tomahawks. All the young men hereabouts do. It's sport. I think *your* head is addled." Then I picked up Anthony and ran from the store.

On the ride home I cried, holding Anthony in front of me on Saxony. For my friend Nancy. For the scalped Myer. For Tecumseh. For Anthony's lost babyhood. And for myself.

In the end, both Black Hoof and Tecumseh had the last laugh on everyone. They joined forces and met in a council with whites sent by our new Governor Kirker.

General Worthington and Daddy went to the council. Simon Kenton was there, too. So was Blue Jacket. My brothers went with the militia.

Daddy told us how the Indians were supposed to stack their arms and not bring them in.

"Tecumseh refused," he said, "but he bore himself well. Everyone respected him. You know that tomahawk he has, with a pipe on one end? He said he needed to carry it. That he might need to use the pipe end of it or the tomahawk end of it before the day was through."

Then, Daddy told us, a parson came up to Tecumseh with a clay pipe and asked to smoke it with him for peace. Tecumseh sniffed it and threw it away.

"We were ready for anything to happen," Daddy said. "But when Tecumseh threw that pipe, both Indians and whites laughed. The tension was broken. Tecumseh then handed his pipe-tomahawk to a white man and joined the council."

"And so what was the outcome of this council?" Mama asked.

"It was decided that Myer was killed by some strange Indians passing through," Daddy said.

"Why couldn't they have decided that before the militia was called out?" Mama asked.

Why, indeed. I thought grown men are all like three-year-old little boys playing with tomahawks. Even Tecumseh.

"So it all ended well then," Mama said.

"Ended?" Daddy asked. "My dear, it is just begun. Governor Kirker has invited Tecumseh and other chiefs to a banquet here in Chillicothe at the end of the month. Everyone will be here. Including Simon Kenton."

CHAPTER 18

I had three weeks to sew a dress that would make me prettier than any woman in Chillicothe.

James's wife Martha helped me cut it out. We worked on it evenings when she came with James and the baby. Then Daddy and James would ride over to General Worthington's to help plan the banquet.

It was blue calico with tiny yellow cornflowers on it. "If only I had some lace for the cuffs and neck," I said.

"Nancy Maxwell has some," Mama said. "I'm sure she'd give it to you."

I hadn't seen Nancy since our set-to. Mama knew of it. They spoke frequently.

"I thought you wanted the prettiest dress in Chillicothe," Mama pushed.

"I'll have the second prettiest dress," I said.

In the end, Martha gave me some lace from an old frock of hers. She showed me a new way to do up my hair, too.

"You should show your face to its best advantage," she said. "You have a classic profile."

I never thought there was anything classic about me. I was still too tall, though I was less clumsy. And no, I was not taken in with a finely turned phrase. But Martha was turning out to be the sister I always wanted. I pondered while we stitched. Friends are found in the oddest places. Sometimes even in one's family.

They were already calling the banquet for the Indian chiefs at General Worthington's house historic. I saw nothing historic about it. But those same people were the ones who called General Worthington's house an elegant seat. So what could you expect?

If the house was elegant at all, it was because George helped build it. They said the architecture takes your breath away. I thought the view of the range of hills west of Chillicothe was to be credited for that.

I knew little about architecture. But I thought that

the way they had the table set with silver and china from Europe and food from all over the old states piled in pyramids was a feat of architecture in itself.

General Worthington's wife had servants dressed all fancylike and walking around offering food on silver trays to people. Like we were too simpleminded to go and fetch it ourselves.

Martha said this was the way they did it back east. She went to school in Boston. I thought, Why are we trying to be like people in the old states? We came out here to start fresh, didn't we?

But I took my morsel of food that the servant offered me, nibbled it like Martha said I was supposed to do, and listened while she told me how fine living is the key to civilization.

Myself, I thought Webster's new spelling dictionary was the key to civilization. But I didn't say it. Because my mouth was full of some strange food that stuck it closed.

"It's liver pâté," Martha said.

She explained to me about liver pâté. I still wasn't sure what it was. But I knew this: it wasn't what *we* do with liver in hog-killing season.

All this went on while we were waiting for the Indians to come in. Tecumseh had given a grand speech outside and the crowd had been spellbound. He was now being congratulated.

I looked around after the speech for Molly Kiser. Would she be here? I'd seen Wabethe under some trees with some other Indian women but not Molly.

Then Martha wanted to go inside. No matter. I couldn't have gotten near Tecumseh if I tried. All the people who in the beginning of the month were accusing him of being a murderer were falling over each other now to get close to him.

All except Nancy Maxwell. She hadn't come. Of course, Mama had asked me to go and ask her to come, as I'd done last time.

"But I know you two have had a falling-out, so I'll let you make your own decision. As we want all our grown children to do," Mama had said.

I'd be sixteen in a week. My decision was that I would not go. Standing there trying to unstick my mouth from the liver pâté, I had some pangs of remorse. Sheriff Maxwell told Mama his wife was sitting alone in her parlor with her rifle across her knees.

The fact that not only Tecumseh was here, but also Chiefs Roundhead, Panther, and Blue Jacket, was simply too much for her. Sheriff Maxwell said she was waiting for them to attack. With three more loaded rifles beside her on the floor.

I wondered about my anger at Nancy Maxwell. Could my heart get stuck, too, with feelings I'd never put in it before? Like my mouth was stuck with liver pâté?

Then the chiefs came up the front stairs and in through the grand double front doors, followed by my daddy and Simon Kenton. The man who wanted to kill Tecumseh. I thought Kenton looked terrible old of a sudden. Or was it just that my heart was turned against him? Then I saw Tecumseh with Governor Kirker.

Tecumseh's attire was plainer than that of the other chiefs. They wore scalp locks, rings in their noses, elaborate headdresses. Their bodies were half naked and oiled. Tecumseh wore his usual deerskin leggings and shirt. Only they were newer and softer. He also wore his silver medallion around his neck and a feather in his red head band.

And he wore his warmest smile when he caught sight of me. As a matter of fact, he stopped right as he and Governor Kirker were passing. "Gal-o-weh girl," he said. He smiled and nodded.

"A lovely young lady," Kirker said. "From one of the finest families here in Chillicothe."

I did not hear Tecumseh's reply. I was busy thinking that if I had an Indian name it would be Breaks Into Pieces. Because that's what my heart did every time Tecumseh smiled at me.

Everyone stuffed themselves silly on the food and acted like seven kinds of fools. There came a moment of crisis, though, for which I think the banquet truly earned its name of historic.

Coffee was served. The Indians were much taken with coffee. George told me that at certain times they have killed for it. No one had to kill for it that day. It was served in great plenty out of a shining silver pot.

The chiefs were served first. Tecumseh, Roundhead, Blue Jacket.

"They haven't served Panther," I whispered to Martha.

"I'm sure it's some kind of protocol," she said.

"What's protocol?"

"The proper way of doing things." And she turned to speak to one of her friends.

Oh. A Boston word. Well, how did they expect Panther to understand a Boston word? There he was, pacing, frowning, chanting to himself, sulking, while people all around me talked and laughed and sipped their coffee.

I turned to one of the fancied-up servants. "Panther needs coffee," I said.

She smiled at me and moved away.

Was I the only one to notice that Panther was mooded up? He'd taken himself to a far corner and was gesturing and waving his arms. His eyes flashed. His feet stamped.

In a moment Tecumseh, Blue Jacket, and Roundhead were at his side. They spoke to him in their own tongue.

Of a sudden, everyone in the room stopped talking to listen to the exchange. The chiefs were speaking very fast in Shawnee. Voices were raised in anger.

Immediately, the whites nearest them moved back and a note of alarm went through the room.

"What is it? What's happened?" James came up to us with a fresh cup of coffee in his hands.

"Panther has no coffee," I told James.

"What?"

"He has no coffee. Quick. Give him yours."

In an instant, James crossed the shining wooden floors, approached the agonized Panther, and held out the delicate china cup of coffee.

Silence. All the chiefs looked at James. Then Panther grinned, took the cup, and held it high. The chiefs all whooped.

Tecumseh stepped forward. "Good people. We are much sorry for the loud noises and stamping of feet. We have not raised our voices in anger. Chief Roundhead, Blue Jacket, and myself have been joking with Chief Panther. We have given him the name of the Coffeeless Chief. He must carry this name now, always."

Everyone laughed and applauded. But I thought it was more out of relief that there was no bloodshed than out of humor.

Martha told me later that the rest of the evening,

Mrs. Worthington personally plied Panther with cup after cup of coffee. And the Indians all thought that a fine joke, too.

I was not there. I'd slipped outside to try to find Molly Kiser.

She saw me coming before I saw her. She and some other Indian women were encamped next to the Worthington barn.

"It's you," she said to me, as if we'd seen each other only last week. She hugged me. "I'd o' knowed you anywheres. My, ain't you the grown-up fancy lady." She fingered the lace on the cuff of my dress. She touched my face.

"Molly, how are you keeping?" She looked older. Her hair was still greasy, but her clothing seemed a little cleaner, perhaps in honor of the occasion. Or was it that I didn't care if it wasn't clean? It made no nevermind, as she herself would say. I was just so glad to see her. And to know that she recognized me.

"I'm keepin'. Been doin' a lot o' travelin'. Look at you. Just look at you, all growed."

"I'll be sixteen next week."

"My." She took me by the hand and introduced me to the three other Indian women. One was Wabethe. I'd never been introduced to her before. "This is my friend Rebecca," she said. "Can we give you some fixin's?" She drew me to a place where two tripods were set up. Good things were bubbling in each pot.

"What are you making?"

"Possum stew and yellow jacket soup."

Yellow jacket soup! Tecumseh had described its merits to me. I always wanted to taste it. But I declined. "No thank you, I've eaten."

Not far away they had a wigewa like the one I'd gone in that day so long ago when Molly had visited with Blue Jacket.

I said hello to the other Indian women. Molly was stirring the yellow jacket soup. She smiled at me. I thought of the elegant fare piled on the tables inside the house.

This smelled better.

Still, I felt ashamed that these women hadn't been invited inside with their men. But they didn't seem to mind. They laughed and joked amongst themselves. They were having a good time, the way only women who work and eat together can. And I envied them. They seemed so much more free than the women in their fancy dresses inside. Myself included.

Once again the comparison between their way of life and ours pulled at my mind. Could I live like this? I knew I couldn't. Not even for yellow jacket soup.

"How's your ma? And your little sister?" Molly asked.

I brought her up to date with the family as if we'd been girlhood friends. Then I smiled shyly. "I never did thank you properlike for saving my sister that time."

She smiled back, showing the missing teeth of a seven-year-old. "Tweren't nothin'. You'd do the same for a body. Wouldn't you?"

"Yes." I took the note out of the pocket of my dress. I'd written it that morning. It was sealed. I'd known the Indians were leaving before first light in the morning. And that I wouldn't get a minute alone with Tecumseh.

"Molly, we're friends, aren't we?" I asked.

"For sure as the hooty owl comes out at night."

"I've kept your secret about the silver mine. Now I'm going to ask you to keep mine. Here." I gave her the note. "It's for Tecumseh. He's my friend, too. I won't be seeing him this trip. And I must get this to him."

She nodded, took the note, and slipped it into her bodice. In her eyes I saw something, some steady unblinking knowledge. "Trust Molly," those eyes said.

I stayed a while more, visiting with her. Then I left.

The note would get to him. Still sealed. I knew that. In it I'd written that he should be careful. That I'd heard Simon Kenton wanted to kill him.

Likely he knew it already. There wasn't much Tecumseh didn't know. But just in case he didn't, there it was. No, he would not have Kenton killed. That wasn't Tecumseh's way. Nor would it start a war between the Indians and whites. If a war was coming, nothing could stop it and this wouldn't push it. I'd given the matter a great deal of thought before penning the note.

And yes, I knew I could trust Molly. It was good to have such a friend.

Only Simon Kenton remained the next morning. The man I did not want to speak with. The man I knew I must speak with. The man who had betrayed me.

He lingered at breakfast with Daddy. Johnnycakes and honey, fish and fruit, ham and biscuits were devoured. Coffee flowed, and still he lingered. He and Daddy were deep in a discussion about petitioning the Kaintuck legislature about something. They did not say what. They talked around it. And Kenton was being Kenton about it. Which means stubborn.

My brothers left. The little ones went to school. I went outside into the lovely September morning to wait. Kenton's horse was saddled and tethered at our gate.

"It's your only recourse," I heard Daddy saying as I went out the door. When Daddy used the word "recourse" I knew it was serious.

I waited for Kenton to come out so I could berate him. I had it all fixed in my head what I was going to say. The words burned inside me. Then James rode up and ruined it.

"His mother is dying in Kaintuck," he told me.

"Whose mother?"

"Don't flummox me, Rebecca. We all know what Bushrod knows. What Simon Kenton said about killing Tecumseh. If you're waiting here to ambush him about it, I'm telling you that Kenton's mother is dying in Kaintuck."

"So he has to kill Tecumseh to make things even?"

"Nobody is going to kill Tecumseh. Nobody wants to start an Indian war. If Tecumseh dies, it will be as he wants to die. In battle."

Tears came to my eyes. "I've a mind to tell Kenton what I think of him, anyway."

"He's lost most of his lands. He's near impoverished by now. He's had reverses."

I wished he would speak plain and not in James language. Reverses? It sounded like a disease, like Kenton needed some cold water root tea.

"Back in Kaintuck he was a rich man," James explained. "He had a thousand acres, and that was only part of what he owned. He's lost it all through bad speculation and failure to pay taxes. Pa's trying to convince him to petition the legislature to remit the forfeiture of his land for taxes. But he's too proud."

More James words. Land. Taxes. What did I care about land and taxes? I turned away.

"Come with me," James said. "Saddle Saxony. I want to show you something."

"I still want to see Kenton when he comes out. I'll not let you keep me from saying my piece, James."

"Did they get to talking about old times yet?"

"No. It's still all about the legislature."

"Then come along. There's plenty of time. Nobody's going to keep you from saying your piece. I just want to make sure you know what piece it is you want to say."

We rode about a mile. In the fine blue-and-gold September morning this was not a chore. Finally, James reined in his horse a little distance from a large tree.

"What do you see?" he asked.

"An old elm."

"When this was Indian territory, Kenton was scouting here. He became separated from the others. The Indians picked up his scent and were pursuing him. They were out to kill him. See that hickory tree next to the elm? There's a wild grapevine that connects the two trees. Kenton had no place to go. So he climbed from the hickory tree to the elm on the grapevine. And stayed there. For seven hours. While the Indians camped underneath. Finally, they gave up searching for him and left."

I looked at the elm. In the quiet field, its branches spread gracefully. Birds twittered in it.

"There hasn't been an expedition against the British or the Indians that was ever raised but he was the most important person in it," James said quietly. "We wouldn't be settled here if not for Kenton. He never captured horses for his own gain. He'd hand them over to those who lost horses to the Indians. And he never struck out at any but hostile tribes who warred against the settlers. Many a settler in Virginia and Kaintuck owes him their life. Now you want to bring pressure to bear on an old man whose reward is impoverishment, you go ahead, Rebecca. You're too old for me to tell you what to do anymore."

And with that, he rode off. I followed. When we got home, Kenton's horse was still tethered to our gate. He and Daddy were just coming outside. He was leaving.

I said my good-byes and watched him ride away. I wish James hadn't said I was too old for him to tell me what to do. The decision to let Kenton go unberated was mine. I didn't say my piece. It was right not to, I know. But doing right doesn't always make you feel good. I felt cheated.

CHAPTER 19

May 1808

All winter I was lonely. I felt the loss, keenly, of those I held dear.

Simon Kenton, yes. Though we'd never been close, I'd admired him, looked up to him, and though I let him go in friendship, he was as one lost to me. Of course, I missed Tecumseh. And then there was Nancy Maxwell.

I did not go to her house for instruction in music or literature anymore. I told Mama I was too old for it. I could read on my own. And Daddy was having a pianoforte shipped from Virginia for our new stone house, which would be ready for us by the end of the summer.

I played the violin for Mama. I wove curtains for the new house, bedsheets, a dress for Ann, who turned nine in April. I planted the kitchen garden in spring and read Shakespeare until my eyes near fell out.

"You're going to become too civilized for us," Mama joked.

I sewed things for James and Martha's new baby, expected in July. I went to Christmas gatherings, frolics, house-raisings, weddings, quilting bees. Since Ann was old enough to help Mama, I did some following on at Martha and James's house. I helped Martha ready for the baby. I relieved her of some tasks. I played with Richard. I was still lonely.

I missed my time with my old teacher. When I saw her at an occasion, she would say polite words to me. I'd think of how she'd sat with her rifle across her knees last year when the Indian chiefs came to Chillicothe. Because she had no son to meet the enemy at the gates. So I'd say polite words back to her.

I'd said polite words to Simon Kenton the day he left, too. I was becoming like James. Was Mama right? Was I becoming too civilized? Could that happen to me?

I was with Sam, making maple sugar one fine day in May, when I looked up and saw a red-tailed hawk screeching overhead. My heart leapt inside me. He's here, I told myself. Tecumseh is here! No sooner did I think it than I saw Ann running across the fields to us.

"Rebecca, Rebecca! Tecumseh's here. He's come to visit!"

I decided Mama *wasn't* right. I was not becoming too civilized. I had understood the appearance of the red-tailed hawk. I had known what he was screeching, "Tecumseh is here! Tecumseh is here!"

"You go on," Sam said. "I can finish up here."

"I'll help you finish," I said. "I don't want to go running just because Tecumseh has decided to favor us with his presence for the first time in eight months."

Sam smiled.

When we did get home, it was late. The family was at supper already. I know I looked a sight, but I washed outside with Sam and went in to table.

Tecumseh stood when I came in. He nodded. "Gal-o-weh girl." He looked at me almost reverently.

No one paid mind. He had always treated me special.

After supper he and Daddy moved to the book room, smoking and talking. George, Sam, and Will were off somewhere. They took John and Andrew with them.

It was clear to me that something was going on. Mama invited me out for a walk with Anthony and Ann.

The May sun had kissed the earth all day, and now the sweetness of that kiss lingered in the evening air.

"Is there trouble?" I asked Mama.

She gave me a sidelong glance. "I hope not, dear." It was all she would say. We walked all the way down to Massie's Creek, Anthony and Ann running ahead of us. When we got back, Mama stopped at the gate and looked at me.

"Your father and I have raised you to know your own mind about things, Rebecca," she said.

"Of course, Mama."

"We can take our children only so far. Then we must let them go on their own course. So far, none of our children has disappointed us."

It sounded serious. I nodded and we went into the house.

Tecumseh and Daddy were still talking in the book room. I saw Ann to bed, lighted a candle, and read a bit. Downstairs, I heard Daddy and Tecumseh, still talking.

In the morning Tecumseh did not breakfast with us. I looked out the window and saw him over his cooking fire by his wigewa. My brothers seemed all turned in on themselves and anxious to get to their chores. There was the usual commotion as Mama got the little ones ready for school and went outside to see them off. I told Daddy I was riding over to James and

Martha's to help her with her kitchen garden. If Tecumseh was too busy to see me, I'd decided, I would be too busy to see him.

"Wait," Daddy said.

I waited.

"I was up late last night talking with Tecumseh." He looked old of a sudden. And sad.

"He's asked for your hand. He's asked to marry you."

The room seemed to tilt around me. I was sure it wasn't the room's fault. The world was tilting. *Marry him?* I was flooded with a warm feeling of completeness, of knowing I would never be unsure of anything again.

It lasted only a minute. Then I thought. *Marry him?* Go and live in an Indian village? In a wigewa? Like the Indian women cooking yellow jacket soup outside General Worthington's house the night of the banquet? Like Molly Kiser?

Mama came back in. I ran to her and hugged her. "Come now," she said, "you've been languishing all winter. And the set-to with Nancy over him. What did you think all that was about?"

"What do I do now, Mama?"

"Rebecca, child," Daddy said, "what you do now is think. Very carefully. Because in your answer is the fate of thousands."

"James, don't put it to her that way," Mama said.

"And what other way is there to put it, then? If she

241

weds him, there will be no more talk of war. It will be the true uniting of the two races. She must be mindful of that."

"And if she doesn't?" Mama asked.

"The choice is hers and hers alone. To be made with her God and her heart. She must pray over it, long and hard. She isn't responsible for the fate of those thousands. No one person should be. Tecumseh swore to me he would not let that be part of it." Daddy paused, then spoke again. "But she should be told of those thousands," he said.

They were still arguing the point, softly, when I slipped out the door. If what they could said to be doing was arguing.

I walked out to our wheat field, where Tecumseh was waiting. Above, the red-tailed hawk circled, screeching, "Thousands! Thousands!"

Tecumseh stood, strong and proud, as I approached.

I looked up into his strong, kind face, into his intelligent, sad eyes. "I don't know what to say," I told him.

He put a finger to his lips. "Gal-o-weh girl say nothing now. Much thinking must be done. Here." He pointed to his head. "And here." He pointed to his heart. "This is not the time to answer."

"What is this the time for then?"

He smiled, took my hand, and drew me toward him. "To go canoeing," he said.

242

* * *

He stayed three days. We spent those golden May days canoeing, playing with Anthony, whose tomahawk throwing pleased him. We walked. We read. He never brought up the subject of marriage, nor did I. He ate with my family, he continued his discussions about treaties and land and his Fort Greenville village with Daddy. He knew the white man wanted his village moved. He knew that for him to keep his people there would mean an outbreak of hostilities.

He did not want hostilities, he said.

So he would move again.

He was considering a place near the Tippecanoe River. The Potawatomies and Kickapoos had invited him to join them there.

He spoke of none of this to me. But to Daddy, who did not advise or question him but just listened.

And there was another thing, right in front of my face as I watched the two favorite men in my life together. I knew Daddy set great store in this friendship. What would happen if I refused Tecumseh? Would the friendship end?

I studied on it as I watched Tecumseh smoke his tomahawk pipe with Daddy. He even made a little one just like it for Anthony when he left.

When he left, he said he would be back in one moon for my answer.

CHAPTER 20

The spring became a mockery to me.

I moved about through it like someone dead. I could not sleep or eat. I did my chores without thinking. I moved amongst my family, seeing them all as if for the first time. They stood out from their background, stark and unreal one moment, grating on my nerves the next, and then as the only source of comfort I had.

No one pushed me into making a decision. My brothers looked wary, as if they hoped I wouldn't ask their opinions. Even James.

Every night when we gathered for prayers, Daddy prayed that I would be moved to come to the right decision.

Whatever it was. No one claimed to know.

"We trust you" was all my parents would say. And they would not be moved, one way or the other, to influence me.

I went about like someone with an ague. I walked alone a lot. I wandered outside in the middle of the night to look at our farm by moonlight, to take solace from the familiar outbuildings, the wheat and cornfields, the fences, even the noise of the hogs and chickens in their pens.

In church on Sunday, when we were singing the familiar hymns, my heart would become so constricted I thought it would stop. And my gaze would shift to the windows, past the patient horses tethered to carriages and wagons, to the familiar fields, while some hymn to God on high floated out and upward on the still air.

I cried a lot. My spirit was cast down.

Then I decided, finally, to talk to the two people who would most likely have something to say on the subject.

"Marry him," Will said, as I expected he would say.

"But what will become of me if we wed?"

"What will become of you if you don't?"

"What of my children? Will they be raised as little savages?"

"They will be raised as you raise them to be."

"Where would we live?"

"Together."

"Will I have to become an Indian woman? Uncivilized?"

"Is he uncivilized?"

"No."

"Anyway, there are worse things," Will said.

"What?" I asked.

He looked at me. "You don't know? You saw me when I lost Elizabeth, and you don't know? Marry him," he said again. "Our true soul mate comes along only once in a lifetime. What happens doesn't matter. Marry him. All I have now that Elizabeth is gone is the fact that we were wed. We didn't wait the way everyone wanted us to. Suppose we'd waited?"

I might have known Will would be no help.

I dismounted Saxony in front of the Maxwell house. It was early of a sweet May evening. In a week Tecumseh would be back.

The place looked deserted. I knew Sheriff Maxwell was off to a meeting of the militia because my brothers were there, too. I needed the place to be deserted. But I knew Nancy would be inside.

At the door I had a moment of misgiving. Suppose she turned me away? Could I bear it? Well, it didn't matter. I could feel no worse than I was feeling now.

I knocked. Once, twice. Oh, please be home, I

246

prayed. I need you. But I didn't know what words I'd say if she was.

Soft footfalls inside. Then the door opened.

She stood there, looking more frail and old than I recollected. Before I had a chance to open my mouth, she reached out her arms to me.

I went to her. She hugged me tight. How foolish I've been, I thought. How foolish. No words are necessary.

She did not say marry him, of course. I did not expect her to. Nor did she say don't marry him. I did not expect that, either. I knew that in this house, where I'd learned to play the pianoforte, to recite Shakespeare, to speak and learn the truth, I could discuss it freely, all the different sides of it. And she would help me study on it.

"You know how I feel about him," she said. "About all of them."

"Yes."

"That's out of the whole cloth. My feelings are from a generation gone past. Yours are from a generation that must learn to live with them. I will think no less of you if you wed him, Rebecca."

We did not speak of the incident in Gowdy's Mercantile. Or the months in between. We just sat right down and took up where we left off.

She got out a piece of paper and pen. She drew a line down the middle of it. "On this side, you will write down your misgivings about the matter," she directed. "On the other side, your reasons for doing it."

She left me there with the paper and pen and went to gather things for tea.

I felt as if I were doing a school lesson. So I set myself to the task. I wrote.

In a little while she returned, served the tea, and held her hand out for the paper. I gave it to her.

"Both sides are equal," she said.

"Yes."

She studied it some more. "There is matter of grave importance on both sides. On the 'in favor of' side you write that such a marriage will unite the races and prevent the bloodshed of thousands. On the 'against' side you write that you don't think you can go to an Indian village and live that kind of life. You would miss your weaving, your books, your church, your *everything*."

"Yes," I said. "But without him, I would die."

She nodded and folded her hands in her lap. "I won't tell you that you won't die if you refuse him. I won't say time will heal. It doesn't. The pain lessens at times, yes, but it never heals. It changes us. And never for the better. It makes out of us what I was in Gowdy's Mercantile a while back with you. And what I was the night of the reception for the chiefs. Angry and bitter and afraid."

I nodded, listening.

"I cannot tell you what to do any more than your parents can. But I would suggest that you name your fears to him. Ask him how you would live. And tell him what you would expect of this union. What would you like to happen?"

I laughed. "I'd like for him to come and live with my people. Farm. Read. Travel and still visit his people, maybe, but live as one of us. Like Simon Kenton does. He travels and meets with the Indians. He's even lived with them from time to time. They all respect him. But he always goes home."

"Tecumseh's home is in their villages," she said.

"He could go there," I answered. "I would wait for him to return."

"Tell him this, then," she said.

"Tell him?"

"Yes. You dishonor him if you don't."

"But what if he doesn't agree? And we then can't wed?"

"What if you wed and this is in your heart and you tell him afterward? Then you dishonor both of you."

CHAPTER 21

June 1808

He came back in June, the sweetest June I recollect. We had half a dozen baby lambs. The fruit trees were laden with blossoms. My roses and geraniums were blooming. No cutworms, no caterpillars to plague us. Moses was father to a new litter of kittens. The air was laden with the fragrance of growing things. You could see God's hand everywhere. Going outside was better than going to church.

He came quietly. One morning I looked out my bedroom window and his wigewa was simply there in the wheat field.

"He's here," George said, coming in from the barn. But they all knew.

"What will you do, Rebecca?" John asked. He was

fourteen. His shoulders were a man's. Will was only thirteen when he was smitten with his Elizabeth. I felt old. The years sat on me. I would be seventeen in October.

"What she has a mind to do," Daddy told him.

"If you don't marry him, he'll start a war against us," Ann said. Out of the mouths of children.

"Hush," Mama told her.

I could not eat. Mama put some food in a basket and walked me to the door. "I have no quote from Franklin for you," she said. "I don't think Franklin had one for such a situation. Just do what is in your heart. And know we stand behind you."

I took the basket and a mug of coffee for Tecumseh and went out the door.

Before I was at the garden gate, George called out to me. I turned to see him standing at the kitchen door. "Yes?" I asked.

He walked to me, slowly. "Rebecca," he said, "you've shined his eyes. Like we do on the hunt. But you can let him go if you want. No one will think less of you."

I wanted to hug him. My big brother. So respectful of me. So caring. I wanted to cry. I did neither. "Thank you," I said.

We rowed to the second bend in the river in my canoe. I did the rowing, he sipped the coffee.

I managed the rapids so well, he grinned. "You do good. Now, maybe you smile for me? And not act like you are going to be burned at the stake?"

He took the paddle from me and guided the canoe to the embankment where the tree had been that he'd cut down. Then he helped me out, and we sat on the log and ate Mama's food.

Meat, biscuits, apples, cheese. He ate ravenously, then bent to drink from the river. I watched him bending over and thought how like a lean, healthy animal he is. His movements are so spare, so sure.

He cupped some water in his hands and brought it to me. He knelt in front of me, holding the water. I was not sure what to do. And then I was. It was an offering.

I leaned my face down and sipped. When I was finished he brought the water closer to me and I dipped my face in. He raised his cupped hands and cooled my face gently with the water, smoothing my brow and hair.

"Thank you." His eyes were shining. George was right.

"This is all I can give you, straw-hair girl," he said solemnly. "The woods, the fields, the streams."

I nodded soberly. "You give yourself," I said.

"You have taken," he said. "You have pulled out my soul."

"I did not mean to take your soul, Tecumtha. No one has a right to take another's soul."

"But it must be given if there is love. As you have given me yours. This is true?" And he regarded me with such a huge sadness, I wanted to cry.

"Yes, this is true."

"I have come to love many white people," he said. "Many have pulled out my soul."

"Who?"

"The one they call Boone. Long-knife captain Clark. Even Simon Kenton. And General Wayne. I have known all these white people and come to see how strong and brave they are. But with these others, always I fought for my soul and got it back. With you, I do not wish to have it back."

I said nothing.

"So now, what is to become of these two pulled-out souls?" he asked.

"Do you still wish to wed me?"

"I wish it more than I wish myself to live until the hunter's moon."

"Then I must tell you my thoughts."

He nodded. His face gave no sign of feeling.

"I love you, Tecumtha. I always have. But I would not dishonor you. I would tell you now that I could not live in an Indian village. I could not become a squaw. I could not live like that." I thought with sadness of Molly Kiser.

"You would not be a squaw. You would be a chief's wife. Everything would be done for you. You would have respect and everything you need. Great honor at all times."

I shook my head. "I couldn't do it, Tecumtha. I need to live as a white woman. I need my children raised as whites. I need to wear my own clothing, cook in my own way, tend to the ways of my household as I've been taught. I need my children to be sprinkled as Christians."

"You say no, then?"

"No. I say you come and live as one of us. Amongst my people. We will have land, a farm. I know you're a great chief. And your people look to you. You may go and travel among them, even live among them, to do what you have to do. But come back to me. And our children. As my husband."

"No chief does this," he said.

"The whites who have pulled out your soul do it. Simon Kenton travels and sees to his business all the time. Daniel Boone did it. And so did General Wayne. He gave his all to the army and hardly ever went home. George Washington did it. He was away from his farm for years at a time. Sometimes Martha, his wife, went to his camp to be with him. Sometimes not."

He nodded. His brown eyes were pensive.

"Does your father do this?"

"No. He doesn't have to. But if he chose to, my mother would be in agreement."

He said nothing. He got up and walked to the river. I stood watching. Above us I saw the red-tailed hawk circling in the sky, screaming.

What was he screaming? I did not know. I had become too civilized. I watched Tecumseh's strong back, saw him as I'd seen him that first day when I was seven years old. As part of the trees, the undergrowth, the landscape. Even part of the river and the sky. Like he belonged there.

I waited for what seemed like a very long time. Then he turned and smiled at me. "Come see the deer, Gal-o-weh girl," he said to me.

I went to stand by him. He took my hand. Across the river, I saw three deer looking at us. "The deer obey the laws of Weshemoneto," he said. "He stays healthy. He has no diseases. He is good to eat. If we are hungry and hunt them, they know it, and come out of hiding for us. Before we kill them, we speak to them, we tell them of the laws and why we need them and remind them that they were created by Weshemoneto to help us fulfill his laws. They are sacred. They know the future. When they die, they go to the Creator, and they take our prayers with them."

I thought of the time I'd gone on the fire hunt with my brothers. And they'd shot the deer for us to eat.

But they hadn't spoken to them first. I liked Tecumseh's way better.

Then he turned his attention to me. "Will you kiss me once, Gal-o-weh girl?" he asked.

"Yes," I said.

So, with the deer still watching us, we kissed. It was gentle and sweet. Then he drew away. His eyes were shining.

"I feel wed to you in this moment," I said. "With the deer as witnesses."

"Then let us make promises. The deer will bring them to Weshemoneto, like our prayers."

"Will you promise," I asked, "that if war comes, that you will throw all your powers against the massacre of women and children? Or men who surrender to you? And not let them be tortured or killed?"

"This I promise," he said. "Will you promise not to disbelieve in me when you hear tales about me that your heart tells you are not true?"

"I promise," I said.

"Then our pulled-out souls are wed."

"Oh, Tecumtha!"

"Don't cry, Gal-o-weh girl. What conditions you ask for marriage, I cannot do. Even if I wished it, I could not do it. My people need me. They are hungry. They are moving now to a new village. I must be with them, always. I must forget my own needs."

I nodded. "But what will happen to us now?" I asked.

"I will speak to your father. I will tell him he and your people have nothing to fear from me. Ever. You will wed some white man some day. And have many children."

"I won't!"

"You must. Or our love will afflict your fine spirit. And dishonor me. And remember, you must not turn away from being a woman. Women are sacred."

"And you? Will you wed?"

"I will stay like the French black robes."

"The priests?"

"Yes. They do not take women for themselves. They stay free and strong to help their people."

"Never wed?"

He smiled. "I have been wed, Rebecca. Two times."

"Oh, Tecumtha!" I wailed.

He took my hand. "I will take you back to your people," he said. "We say good-bye here. Now. And I will not come again. This cannot be."

Overhead, the red-tailed hawk was screeching again. This time I understood. "Good-bye! Good-bye!" Never had I known such searing, tender sorrow. My heart was fair to bursting inside me.

EPILOGUE

October 1813

"Rebecca, Rebecca! There's an Indian down by the creek!"

I heard Anthony's voice and his running footsteps and bestirred myself from my loom.

He came bursting through the door. At nine, Anthony did not enter. He burst.

"An Indian?" My heart seemed to stop.

"Down by the creek. Looks like a squaw. She's watching our house!"

I grabbed a shawl, threw it around my shoulders, made sure baby Ann was sleeping in her cradle, and went outside. The late October air was like wine. You could drink it.

Our house was new, and this was the first year for

my kitchen garden. "Anthony, you were supposed to be picking the last of the beans," I said. Sprout, one of Moses' kittens, followed me.

"I did."

"You've dropped them all over the ground."

"I got scared when I saw the Indian woman."

"Nonsense. There's nothing to be afraid of."

"An Indian squaw, Rebecca!" His upturned face, full of freckles, was filled with the excitement of it. "She's down there by the creek with George."

I shaded my eyes. It was true. My husband, George, was talking with an Indian squaw by the creek. She was alone, except for her horse. I shivered, though the October sun was warm.

Then I heard the screech of the red-tailed hawk overhead in the bright blue sky. *What was he saying?*

But I knew. I felt it in my bones. I am not that civilized yet, though I have been wed since last December to my very civilized cousin, Pennsylvania George Galloway. And he and my brothers built this lovely home for us, just five miles from Daddy's place. And my baby, Ann, just a month old, lies asleep in her cradle.

"Who do you think she *is*?" Anthony was saying.

"We'll find out, soon enough."

"Shall I ride to Pa's and ask Will and Sam or John and Andrew to come?"

"No. They've enough to do keeping two farms with the others away. My George can handle it."

In a little while my husband came up the hill. But the Indian woman stayed there.

"Rebecca, I have news," he said.

"Yes, George."

"Tecumseh is dead."

He laid the words at my feet. I was not surprised, for the red-tailed hawk had told me the tidings a few moments ago, screeching overhead. "Tecumseh is dead! Tecumseh is dead!"

But I was shocked. And the shock seemed to come up through my feet, from the very earth beneath me. Even as the earth was taken with shock in the great quake that happened two years ago, the quake Tecumseh had predicted, that was a sign that all the Indians should unite behind him. A real sign, a real prophecy. Not one he got from the *Kentucky Almanac*.

"Rebecca, do you hear me?"

"I hear you, George."

"Dead!" Anthony's face fell. "Who killed him?"

"It happened the first week in October. In the Battle of the Thames. At least that's what *she* told me. Says she's passing by. And thought you would want to know."

"Who *is* she?" Anthony asked.

George tousled his hair. Anthony had been living with us since Mama died a year ago August. He'd been a great help. Ann stayed home. She's fourteen and following on. She looks well to the ways of the new house for Daddy.

"Says she knew Blue Jacket before he died," George answered. Blue Jacket had died of a fever over two years ago.

Then George put his hand on my arm. "Rebecca, are you all right?"

He knew about me and Tecumseh. I was not sorry I married George. I loved him. A different kind of love than I had for Tecumseh. George is a steady, good man. He, too, thinks women are sacred. But we do not pull each other's souls out. Oh, there is nothing wrong with that kind of love. But there is much to be said for loving and leaving the souls in place. And it would please Tecumseh to know I've not turned away from being a woman.

Just as it pleased me when we heard about Fort Meigs in Ohio.

Fort Meigs. I shudder to think on it. It wasn't bad enough that the British and Indians killed so many American soldiers in that battle. American soldiers who surrendered were made to run a gauntlet to get to the gates of old Fort Miamis, where they were promised protection, once they ran the gauntlet.

So they ran, while the Chippewa Indians clubbed, beat, and bayoneted them to death.

Those Americans who did manage to make it through to the fort were being butchered by the Chippewas.

Tecumseh fought under British general Henry

Proctor in that battle. But he was not at the surrender. A runner brought the news to him of what was happening.

Tecumseh galloped on his fine horse to the site. Bodies were all over, and Proctor, who stood there watching the slaughter, refused to give the Americans protection against the maddened Chippewas.

Tecumseh bellowed at the Indians, shaming them, reminding them how they had agreed in council that prisoners were not to be tortured or slain. "You want to kill prisoners, do you?" he challenged "Then you must kill me first. Then do as you please."

The Chippewas backed down. Then Tecumseh sent Proctor from the fort, saying he was not fit to command, that he should go and put on a petticoat.

It happened in May. Word came to us in June.

Tecumseh had kept his promise to me.

We know about it because Bushrod Sheley was there. Bushrod Sheley who boasted to me how Simon Kenton said they must kill Tecumseh. Bushrod was one of the prisoners saved by Tecumseh's actions. Nancy Maxwell's nephew. He came to Chillicothe and told us of it in his own words. Told, not bragged. I don't think Bushrod Sheley will ever brag about anything again. And Nancy Maxwell cried when he told it.

"I'm fine, George," I answered my husband. "Who shot Tecumseh?"

"Nobody knows. Though half a dozen American officers are laying claim to it."

"Was it quick? Did she say?"

"Shot in the heart. One ball. Yes."

I sighed. "Are they sure it was him?"

"They say he was over six feet. Dressed like an ordinary Indian brave. One side of his face painted black, the other red."

Yes, I thought. The black of death on one side, the red of war on the other. As his father, Hard Striker, had looked when he died in battle. And his older brother Chiksika. So he knew he was going to die, then. He was prepared.

Oh, Tecumseh! And to think, I could have prevented this!

No, I must not think on it. I must swallow those words. No one person could have prevented what they are now calling the Second War with the British. Or the War of 1812. Though it is 1813 and it is still going on. This war has many causes. But they like to blame it on the Indians.

"Rebecca, you should go inside and sit down," George said.

I looked up into his dear face and smiled. "How long will this war go on, George?"

"I don't know. Maybe it will end now."

I was weary of it. A year and a half we've had of war

now. James gone off fighting. Brother George, too. Will and Sam talking about going. At fifty-eight Simon Kenton had gone. His son, Simon, Jr. had been captured by Indians.

I waved at the Indian squaw. She waved back. "Did you invite her in, George?"

He shrugged. "She didn't want to come."

I heard the baby crying in the house. I looked up. And for a moment a darkness came over the sun. As if we were having an eclipse. And I saw myself, a gap-toothed little girl, dropping her basket of beans and running into the log house to call her mama.

"Mama! Mama, there's an Indian out there watching us!"

Down through the years I heard the cry. Or was it the hawk, still circling overhead?

Anthony's basket of beans, strewn all over the path of the kitchen garden, was a sign, I was sure of it. A sign that Tecumseh was at peace now. Things had come full circle. And he wanted me to know it.

Oh, Tecumtha, I will never forgotten.

"George, will you see to the baby?" I asked.

"Of course."

"Anthony, pick up those beans. Every last one of them. We'll be having them for supper."

"Oh, all right." He followed George back toward the house.

I turned in the direction of the creek. I sighed and took one last look up at the circling hawk. It settled in an elm tree, watching.

As it watched, I drew my shawl around my shoulders against the October chill and walked down the hill to the creek to greet my old friend Molly Kiser.

Author's Note

All my historical novels are a mixture of fact and fiction. I use as much fact as is available to me. The fiction comes about when I run into brick walls in the research, as I did with the lives of Rebecca Galloway's siblings. Except for James, there was a scarcity of fact beyond the days of their births, deaths, and marriages. We know James was named surveyor of the Virginia Military District, that he married Martha Townsley, wrote for the *Freeman's Journal* under the name of Pioneer Junior, was a major in the militia and a respected personage in and around Chillicothe. Yet history tells us little about Rebecca's other siblings.

We do know that Will married and his wife died a

year later. (I have Elizabeth Pomeroy as a bound girl for the sake of drama.)

So I had to invent the personalities and interests of the others. Thus I have George working in wood, telling stories, and being the gentle eldest son, Sam raising dogs, and Will going to pieces when Elizabeth dies. Likewise I gave little Ann, John, Andrew, and Anthony their own personalities, as well as Rebecca's mother and father and all the other people who once lived and walk through the pages of this book.

Because the pioneers of Ohio were either too busy to write or didn't know how, I had to reach out in several directions to get sufficient background for this book. I read everything I could get on the Galloway family, on Greene County, and Old Chillicothe, as sent to me from my two major sources, the Greene County Historical Society and the Greene County Room of the Greene County Public Library. Then I read every book I could get my hands on about pioneer life in the old Northwest.

There were actually at least five villages named Chillicothe in Ohio. The Chillicothe referred to in the story is Old Chillicothe in Greene County. I have incorporated some elements of Chillicothe in Ross County into my depiction of the Greene County town of the same name. It was really the Ross County Chillicothe that was made the state capital.

How true is the story of Tecumseh, the great Shawnee chief, asking a sixteen-year-old white pioneer girl to marry him?

In his wonderful book, *The Frontiersmen*, Allan W. Eckert incorporates this romance. Then in a follow-up book, *A Sorrow in Our Heart*, he runs a disclaimer in the footnotes concerning it. In *Panther in the Sky*, another wonderful book about Tecumseh, author James Alexander Thom deals with the romance from his own perspective. He has Rebecca Galloway assuming Tecumseh wants to marry her because he has paid her so much attention, because he has given her gifts in the manner of a white man who is courting.

Clearly the actuality of the romance is up for conjecture, but I have found more evidence that it happened than evidence to dispute it.

In *Old Chillicothe*, a Shawnee and pioneer history by William Albert Galloway, A.M., M.D., LL.D., a Galloway descendant, the author chronicles not only the romance of Rebecca and Tecumseh but relates the story of the "blossoms" on the tree that Tecumseh explained to Rebecca were the "Indian's secret" and how the Indian took the powder from the blossoms for a painkiller.

The scene in my book in which Tecumseh chops down the tree to assure Rebecca that she and her people "will never have need of it from us," is my own, taken from a quote from Tecumseh as related in *Old Chillicothe*: "The tree and the flowers shall be destroyed that no harm may come to you or your family. It is the pact of peace. Now you are our care, no harm can come to you."

In *Old Chillicothe* I also found Indian Joe and the Maxwells. Sheriff Maxwell did start the first newspaper in the old Northwest. He did write *Maxwell's Code*, the only law before Ohio became a state. His house was built half a mile from his property line. Nancy Maxwell did fight off the Indians at the fort at Grave Creek in Virginia with the help of Elizabeth Zane. But she did not lose a child there. (Although Indians were known, in the heat of battle, to smash babies against trees and kill them.) I created Nancy Maxwell's character and wrote her to be as many women of the time.

From my research it seems that Rebecca Galloway did teach Tecumseh about literature and the proper way of reading and writing. He already knew English when he came to visit the Galloways. How much he knew about writing, nobody knows.

The fight at the courthouse really happened. Mr. Townsley, father of Martha, really did open the first school. Reverend Armstrong really did cross the creek on stilts. And Molly Kiser was the interpreter for Blue Jacket when he and his men met at the Galloways' with the whites seeking information about the silver mine.

The story of Blue Jacket once being known as Marmaduke Van Swearingen and how he joined the

Shawnees is taken from history. So is everything about Tecumseh, even the timetable of the trips he took. That is, I don't have him anywhere in this book where he wasn't, in history, at the time. His boyhood village was on the land the Galloways chose for their "improvement." He was a prophet in that he did predict certain events. It is, however, up for conjecture whether he learned about the eclipse from the Galloways and their books or if he actually predicted it.

But he did later predict the terrible earthquake of 1811 in the place where the Ohio River met the Mississippi, an earthquake that had effects in Kentucky, Tennessee, Arkansas, Missouri, Illinois, Indiana, Alabama, and Mississippi territories. This same earthquake was taken as a sign by the Indians.

The incident related by Nancy Maxwell of how Tecumseh spied in the fort in Cincinnati is true. The business about his brother, "the Prophet," having a vision and becoming a moral authority for the Shawnees is true. The death dance for Alexander McKee and the story about McKee's deer goring him is true, as is the witch hunt among the Delaware Indians and the hysteria about the white man's dogs and cats and the Indians' intentions to kill them. Eventually, the Indians returned them to their owners.

Tecumseh did come to Chillicothe to make speeches, invited by the governor to quell the fear of the people about Indian aggression. The historic banquet at

Adena, the house of General Thomas Worthington, happened as I depicted it, with the Indian chiefs in attendance and Chief Panther being overlooked in the serving of coffee and taking it as an offense.

Tecumseh did give Rebecca gifts, including a canoe. And he did keep his promise to Rebecca not to kill or torture prisoners taken in battle, as the evidence of his actions at Fort Meigs in Ohio shows us. When a runner came and told him that American soldiers who had surrendered were not only being made to run a gauntlet but were being clubbed and bayoneted by the Chippewas, under the authority of British General Henry Proctor, Tecumseh immediately rode to the site and stopped the slaughter, reminding the Chippewas how they had agreed not to kill prisoners and told them "kill me first." Then he lashed out at Proctor, told him he was fit only to put on a petticoat, and sent him from the fort, assuming command.

Tecumseh did die in the Battle of the Thames. Nobody knows who shot him. In my book I have him writing "we have immediately return our prayers to the Great Spirit above, for you, and *will never forgotten* your goodness towards us . . ." This is taken from his letter to Governor Edward Tiffin on the twentieth of March 1806.

The tale of how Rebecca's father was called to fight in the Revolution is true, as is the story of the bullet he still carried in his neck, put there by Simon Girty, and the senior Galloway's ability to tell the weather by the pain the wound gave him.

According to James Galloway Sr.'s Revolutionary War Pension Application, dated June 7, 1832, he served at Trenton, Princeton, and New Brunswick, New Jersey, the Battle of Long Island, Paulus Hook and Bergen County (New Jersey), Valley Forge, Pennsylvania, then after the war was ordered out west on an expedition against the Indians under the command of General George Rogers Clark.

The Scottish history of the Galloway family is all true. And they did migrate from Kentucky to Ohio because they did not believe in slavery. Brother James did travel back to Kentucky with his father at the time I depict it, to secure a minister for their community, bringing back the Reverend Robert Armstrong. The younger Galloway children were not baptized until they returned, and the first religious ceremony in their community was held in the Galloway barn.

My rendition of the pioneer wedding is taken from research, as is the fire hunt on which Rebecca and her brothers "shined the eyes" of the deer. Research also gave me the sad story of how the girl Phemy's horse died on the trip to Ohio, although Phemy herself is a fictitious character. More research yielded information on what the pioneers grew, what kind of trees were on their land, how many barrels of sap make a pound of sugar, and everything else about their life and surroundings.

Everything about the background of Indian scout, pioneer, and Galloway friend Simon Kenton is true. His interaction with the family members is of my own making although he and Rebecca's father fought together in the campaign of 1782, under General George Rogers Clark. I took artistic license with the trip Kenton made west with Will Galloway. He actually took this trip and spied on Tecumseh at Stony Creek Council, but he had others with him.

The killings of James Harrod and Waw-wil-a-way happened exactly as I depicted them. Even the business about Claudia, the pig who could read and write, is taken from research about Chillicothe.

Rebecca Galloway did marry her cousin, Pennsylvania George Galloway, and did live five miles from her original home, as I have in the epilogue. She did take in her little brother Anthony after her mother died. Did Molly Kiser come back to visit her after Tecumseh was killed? Did the red-tailed hawk really make an appearance to announce Tecumseh?

I like to think so. And my liking to think so, my hunting down and interpreting the hundreds of dry facts I located in books, original papers, family trees, personal letters, pension applications, regional histories, and personal accounts is what makes my historical novels.

Acknowledgments

I am indebted to Joan Baxter, Executive Secretary of the Greene County Historical Society in Xenia, Ohio, for all her help in supplying me information and reading material about the Galloway family, as well as advising me of other directions to go for more research.

Thanks also goes to Catherine Wilson, Library Associate in the Greene County Room of the Greene County Public Library, Xenia, for her patience in photocopying and sending me reading material about Greene County and the Galloway family.

No historical novelist could possibly write anything without the factual books written on the subject he or she is pursuing. Much of the knowledge about pioneer life in this book was gleaned from reading.

Those who compiled the original academic books and papers can never be thanked properly.

Nearer to home I must once again thank the staff of my local library, the Bridgewater branch of the Somerset County Library system in New Jersey, for their patience in getting me books on intralibrary loan. The same thanks is due the staff of the Raritan Valley Community College in my home town of Branchburg.

My appreciation also goes to Regina Griffin for her input, to Karen Grove and Anne Dunn for their assistance, and to Brenda Bowen and Scholastic for their faith in me. And, as always and ever, to my beloved son, Ron, for leading me in to the field of history and for the use of his tremendous library on American and military history.

Bibliography

Bond, Beverley W., Jr. *The Civilization of the Old North-west*. New York: AMS Press, 1934, 1969.

Bowen, Catherine Drinker. *John Adams and the American Revolution*. Boston: Little, Brown and Company, 1950.

Byrd, Walter J. *History of Greene County and the Galloway Family*. Xenia, Ohio, Greene County Room, Greene County District Library, Xenia, Ohio.

Colerick, E. Fenwick. *Adventures of Pioneer Children or, Life in the Wilderness*. Cincinnati, Ohio: Robert Clarke & Co., 1888.

DeVerter, Ruth Hendricks. *Our Pioneer Ancestors, Scott and Galloway*. Baytown, Tex.: 1959.

Dills, R. S. *History of Greene County, Together with Historic Notes on the Northwest and the State of Ohio.* Dayton, O.: Odell & Mayer, 1881.

Eckert, Allan W. *A Sorrow in Our Heart, The Life of Tecumseh.* New York: Bantam Books, 1992.

————. *The Frontiersmen.* New York: Bantam Books, 1970.

Ellet, Elizabeth F. *Pioneer Women of the West.* Freeport, N.Y.: Books for Libraries Press, 1852, reprinted 1973.

Galloway, Margaret Wilson. *The Galloway Family.* Ann Arbor, Michigan: Edwards Brothers, 1940.

Galloway, William Albert. *Old Chillicothe.* Xenia, O.: The Buckeye Press, 1934.

Griffiths, D., Jr. *Two Years in the New Settlements of Ohio.* March of America Facsimile Series Number 73, University Microfilms, Inc. Ann Arbor, Michigan, 1966.

Havinghurst, Walter. *The Heartland, Ohio, Indiana, Illinois, 1673–1860.* New York: Harper and Row, 1956.

Jones, N. E., M. C. *The Squirrel Hunters of Ohio, or Glimpses of Pioneer Life.* Cincinnati, Ohio: The Robert Clark Co., 1898.

Larkin, Jack. *The Reshaping of Everyday Life 1790–1840.* The Everyday Life in America Series, HarperPerennial. New York: HarperCollins, 1988.

Robinson, George F. *History of Greene County, Ohio*. Chicago: S. J. Clarke Publishing Company, 1902.

Thom, Dark Rain. *Kohkumthena's Grandchildren, The Shawnee*. Indianapolis, Indiana: Guild Press of Indiana, 1994.

Thom, James Alexander. *Panther in the Sky*. New York: Ballantine Books, 1989.

Van Every, Dale. *Our Country Then, Tales of Our First Frontier*. New York: Henry Holt, 1958.

ABOUT THE AUTHOR

Ann Rinaldi is the acclaimed author of six ALA Best Books for Young Adults, including the IRA Young Adult Choice *In My Father's House*, and *Wolf by the Ears*, an ALA "Best of the Best" Books for Young Adults and winner of the Pacific Northwest Young Reader's Choice Award. She has also received the Daughters of the American Revolution Award for her outstanding work. Ms. Rinaldi lives in Somerville, New Jersey, with her husband.